Project Dopa

Project Dopa

ERIC AQUINO

Printed in the United States of America
Published in Hellertown, PA
Cover design by Anna Magruder
Library of Congress TO COME
ISBN TO COME

For more information or to place bulk orders, contact the author or the publisher at Jennifer@ BrightCommunications.net.

To Chela

Foreword

When you open the pages of Project Dopa, you'll find yourself in a world that feels at once unsettlingly familiar and wholly imagined - a world of pandemics, survival, and the unrelenting human search for hope. On the surface, it is a page-turning thriller of EMTs, outbreaks, and even the undead. But at its heart, this is a book about resilience, about community, and about what it means to live fully in the face of uncertainty.

Eric Aquino, known to many as the Trembling EMT, has spent his career and much of his life on the front lines responding to emergencies, founding the Gray Strong Foundation, creating spaces for connection, and navigating his own Parkinson's diagnosis. The grit and urgency of the first responder, the intimate knowledge of Parkinson's symptoms and struggles, and the determination to build community when the world fractures are not imagined. They are Eric's truth, woven into a story that dares to ask profound questions in the guise of fiction.

As the story unfolds, we follow characters who discover that Parkinson's may paradoxically hold a key to survival. The novel draws us into the sci-entific mystery and the moral dilemmas it creates: what if the same biology that grants immunity against an unspeakable threat is also the one that strips away certainty about the future? What if a cure could save millions from Parkinson's but ex-pose them to something even more dangerous?

This tension, both thrilling and deeply human, reflects the paradoxes that so many in our commu-nity know well: hope and fear, vulnerability and strength, limitation and possibility. Eric has writ-ten not only a work of imagination but also a med-itation on the choices and connections that define us. The global support networks, the persistence of compassion, and the courage to keep moving forward surge through these pages as strongly as any plot twist.

It is an honor to introduce Project Dopa. May you find in it the suspense of a good story, and the inspiration of a life lived boldly and authentically. Eric reminds us that while we cannot control the circumstances we inherit, we can always choose how we respond, how we connect, and how we live well today.

Polly Dawkins
Executive Director, Davis Phinney Foundation

Chapter 1: Normal World

Alex woke with a start to the familiar wail of ambulances racing past his first-floor window. Times like these, he wished he lived a little higher up in the seven-story apartment building, which sat directly above a bodega on the corner of 179th Street and Walden Avenue in the heart of the Bronx.

The prewar, brick building had weathered decades of change in the vibrant neighborhood. Its facade had knitted into a patchwork of faded red and brown hues, adorned by fire escapes scaling its walls and laundry lines stretching between its windows.

At street level, the bodega's colorful awning announced "Sandwiches, Lotto, Cold Beer" in bold, red letters. Alex recalled how a steady stream of locals used to move in and out of the shop, greeting each other warmly or pausing to chat outside. But that was before the world changed seemingly overnight.

Across the street from the bodega was a small park dotted with benches and chess tables, and Alex remembered the animated, elderly men who would play dominoes and argue about sports.

Stray cats would lounge under the trees while pigeons pecked at nearby crumbs and scraps.

Walden Avenue, a one-way street running north and south, intersected with 179th Street, which was lined with similar brick apartment buildings interspersed with mom-and-pop shops, hair salons, and once-crowded discount stores with racks of clothing and household goods that would spill out onto the sidewalks.

Alex recalled how the scent of sizzling meat from a taco truck parked up the block would mingle with exhaust fumes from idling trucks and incense drifting from botanica storefronts. In his mind, he could still hear the reggaeton and salsa music thumping from passing cars, providing a spontaneous soundtrack to the neighborhood's unending dance between tradition and change.

Towering above it all, the 4 train would rumble along its elevated tracks on Jerome Avenue, ferrying passengers to and from the busy hub of activity below. Life in this corner of the Bronx had pulsed with a rhythm all its own, at once gritty and colorful, a tapestry woven from threads of every culture and each hardship endured in the crucible of shared experience.

Alex glanced at the calendar on his nightstand: March 24, 2030. It had been ten long years since the pandemic had begun. Ten years of living like this.

With a sigh, Alex rose and went through his morning ritual—making breakfast and gathering his mask and gloves. His fridge looked sparse again. *I'll have to venture to the grocery store soon—if this area isn't under quarantine,* he thought.

As Alex settled at the kitchen table with his bowl of cereal, he caught his reflection on the small, darkened TV screen on the counter. He did a double take for a moment, struck by his uncanny resemblance to an older version of Alfonso Ribeiro when he played Carlton Banks on the classic *The Fresh Prince of Bel-Air*.

Alex chuckled, remembering how much he loved that show growing up. Carlton's preppy style, goofy dance moves, and relentless optimism always made him smile, no matter how tough things were in the neighborhood.

Looking closer at his reflection, Alex mused on the similarities—the high cheekbones, mischievous glint in the eyes, cheesy grin. He might have a few more gray flecks in his hair and a couple additional lines around his eyes than Carlton, but the resemblance was still striking.

Alex turned on the TV in his kitchen, reflexively tuning it to the twenty-four-hour news network. He only half-listened as he shoveled cereal into his mouth, but the droning updates from the dispassionate anchor still seeped into his consciousness.

As the blonde, blue-eyed anchor monotonously recited the latest pandemic case numbers, lockdown extensions, and business closures, Alex studied her facial expressions. Her wide–eyed, faux sincerity and pursed-lip concerned look seemed staged and emotionless.

But underneath, Alex glimpsed her true exhaustion with fear-fueled story cycles. The anchor's voice conveyed the drained spirit of a hostage reading demands—flat, robotic, stripped of humanity.

How many months now had she repeated the same litany of tragedy without respite? The sheer weight of accumulated horrors reported would crush anyone's empathetic reserves. Compassion fatigue was inevitable.

Alex suspected his own voice sounded similarly depleted after too many days on the frontlines, witnessing immense suffering and desperation. Each time the ambulance radio crackled urgently to life, he sensed he was reaching the bottom of his well of hope.

Was this the emotional state the endless pandemic would leave everyone in—numb, muted, and bone-weary? When this long nightmare finally ended, would anyone remember what "normal" behaviors used to feel like?

Turning off the TV, with the anchor's dreary drone still echoing in his mind, Alex glanced out his kitchen window to see faint sunlight hinting at life still stirring. People had to hold onto those small graces wherever they appeared until morale could be restored.

Some flicker of positivity still lived in quiet moments of humanity that all the ominous newscasts forgot to mention. It fell to ordinary people to rekindle those faint embers, reviving spirits and dreaming of futures outside the camera frame.

After draining his cereal bowl, Alex started his remote training at his makeshift office—the kitchen table. He missed the social interaction of his old training room, but virtual happy hours were the only off-duty camaraderie permitted these days. Alex was grateful to be employed. A decade into the pandemic, most businesses that remained struggled to stay afloat.

The morning dragged on watching video debriefs and responding to emails. Around noon, Alex's phone buzzed with a text from his friend Emily. "Want to meet for lunch? The Spanish place on Jerome Ave reopened with limited hours and seating. Dying for some real food and human contact!"

Alex hesitated, weighing the risks. In-person gatherings were still strongly discouraged, but the thought of escaping his apartment for a restaurant meal and some much-needed social interaction was tempting.

He texted back, "Great, but R U sure it's safe?"

Emily replied quickly, "They're being super careful—masks required, tables spaced apart, sanitizing between seatings. I think we'll be okay. I really miss you!"

Alex felt a pang of longing for the easy camaraderie he and Emily once shared. Before the pandemic, they'd often grabbed lunch together on his breaks, swapping stories and laughing over plates of *arroz con pollo* or fresh tamales. Looking around his silent apartment, the prospect of a shared meal in a lively neighborhood spot felt like a lifeline to normalcy.

"I'm in," he typed back. "Meet U in 20?"

"Perfect!" Emily responded. "Can't wait to catch up properly. See you soon!"

Alex pocketed his phone and gathered his mask, gloves, and sanitizer. His stomach growled, anticipating the savory scents and flavors that would greet him on Jerome Avenue. For a brief moment, he allowed himself to imagine that life had returned to normal—that he and Emily could linger over lunch like old friends in old times, without fear hanging over every word.

But the illusion faded as Alex stepped out onto the unusually quiet street. With a determined stride, he set off toward the restaurant, heart lightened by the promise of connection amidst the uncertainty. He walked one short block, then down the steps to the train. When he got off at the next stop, he saw Emily already waiting for him at the bottom of the stairs from the platform. Their destination, Maria's, was just a few stores down from the station.

As the friends walked together, a slight awkwardness hung in the air. It had been so long since they'd seen each other in person, and their usual easy banter felt stilted behind stuffy cloth masks. They didn't say much during the short walk, but the shared anticipation of a good meal and the company of an old friend was palpable.

When Alex and Emily entered the restaurant, they were greeted by the comforting aromas of simmering stews and frying meats. The once-bustling dining room was quiet, with only a handful of well-spaced-apart tables occupied. Diners struggled to talk with their masks on while waiting for their meals.

Alex and Emily opted for a booth by the window, where they could watch the life of the city outside. Even with the world so changed, seeing the ebb and flow of passersby on familiar streets and trains rumbling along the elevated tracks was reassuring.

Their server, a friendly older woman they recognized from previous visits, came over to take their order.

"I'll have the lunch special," Alex said, looking forward to a hearty sancocho stew filled with tender cuts of meat, starchy yuca, and fragrant herbs.

"Ditto," Emily said, her smile obscured by her mask, yet lighting up her eyes.

As Alex and Emily waited for their meals, they relaxed into conversation.

"What's new?" Alex asked with genuine interest.

"My school has been virtual for what feels like forever now," Emily shared. "It's been hard adapting to a virtual classroom—especially with the little ones I teach."

"I can't even imagine," Alex said sympathetically. *Teachers aren't paid nearly what they're worth, especially now,* he thought, grateful for his work as an EMT. "My job has the usual challenges, but it is also more rewarding than ever. People seem so grateful for our help."

The arrival of the sancocho brought a welcome pause. *These masks work pretty well! Usually I can smell the plate coming from the kitchen,* Alex thought. Grateful for the excuse to remove their masks, Alex and Emily slowly savored each spoonful, letting the comforting flavors and textures transport them to memories of more carefree times.

Between bites, they reminisced about shared memories and conjured up dreams for the future, their laughter punctuating the subdued atmosphere. For a moment, the heaviness of the pandemic lifted, replaced by the simple joy of good food and even better company.

As Alex and Emily finished their stew, mopping up the last drops with crusty bread, Alex felt a sense of renewed connection and hope. *I've really missed this. I hope things open more so we can do this more often.* No matter how much the world might change, these small moments of togetherness would always be a balm for the soul.

"This is my treat," Alex said when the waitress dropped off their check.

"Well ... okay ..." Emily protested weakly.

"Here we go again," Alex muttered as he re-donned his mask. He peeled two $20 bills from his wallet, then set them on the table to cover the meals and a generous tip. *She's working harder than ever for fewer tips,* he thought. The friends left the restaurant, walked past the stores back to the station, then ascended the steps together.

At the point where their paths split, Alex said, "It was great to catch up." He considered offering a hug, then decided against it. *No hugging allowed!*

"Thank you for the wonderful visit—and the delicious meal," Emily said. "Let's do this again soon."

Alex walked toward the left track while Emily headed to the right—back to their apartments in opposite directions. As Alex rode the train back home, he carried the warmth of friendship and the resilience of a community that would always find ways to come together, even in the darkest of times.

Still buoyed by the warmth and normalcy of his lunch with Emily, Alex decided to take a detour on his way home. Just a few blocks away from where he hopped off the train, hidden behind an unassuming storefront, lay a secret speakeasy that had become Alex's go-to spot for clandestine socializing during the pandemic.

With a furtive glance over his shoulder, Alex slipped into the unmarked entrance and descended a dimly lit staircase. At the bottom, he knocked three times on a heavy wooden door, and a slot at eye level slid open.

"Open sesame," Alex offered the password, then waited as the door swung inward, admitting him into the cozy, lamp-lit interior.

The speakeasy was a throwback to a bygone era with plush velvet couches, antique movie posters, and a well-stocked bar. But instead of illicit alcohol, the patrons here sought a different kind of forbidden pleasure—human connection.

Alex nodded to a few familiar faces as he made his way to a sectioned-off area where a projector was set up for a movie screening. He settled into an overstuffed armchair, grateful for the chance to lose himself in a story and the company of kindred spirits.

As the opening credits rolled, Alex felt the tensions of the day melt away. In this secret haven, he could forget about the pandemic raging outside and the constant isolation it imposed. For a few precious hours, he could laugh, chat, and share in the communal experience of storytelling.

During intermission, Alex struck up a conversation with a small group of young men gathered at the bar.

"Bob, what's new?" Alex greeted a young businessman he had met a few weeks before at the speakeasy.

"Nothing—as usual," Bob replied, sipping his Manhattan. "I'm grateful for this joint, but it's the same-old-same-old. Wish we could find other places to meet."

"Me too," Alex said with a heavy sigh. "It's hard to maintain old friendships, let alone make new ones with all these rotten rules."

"The new normal sucks," said Josh, a former stockbroker, now work-at-home writer, as the group moved from the bar back to their seats to watch the rest of the movie

As the night wore on, Alex felt his spirits lift even higher. The lunch with Emily had been a reminder of the power of one-on-one connection, but this speakeasy represented something larger—a community finding ways to support and uplift each other in defiance of the crisis.

After the final movie scene faded to black and the lights came up, Alex lingered a while longer, savoring the afterglow of laughter and conversation. He knew that soon he would have to return to the solitary confines of his apartment, but for now, he could carry this feeling of belonging with him.

As Alex made his way to the speakeasy exit, he nodded again to friends and even shook a few hands.

"Later, friend," he said to Bob, who was reluctantly putting back on his mask and coat.

"Till next movie night," Bob replied.

With a final round of thanks and goodbyes, Alex slipped back out into the quiet street with his heart full and his resolve strengthened. No matter how long this pandemic might last, he knew that the human spirit would always find a way to connect, to light up the darkness.

As Alex breathed in the night air through his mask, he felt a bittersweet mixture of emotions wash over him. The evening's camaraderie and laughter had temporarily eased his loneliness, filling him with a sense of warmth and connection.

But as the other patrons began to disperse into the night, Alex's thoughts turned to his mother, isolated in a nursing home across the city. The pang of guilt that struck him was as sharp as it was sudden. *I hate that she's all alone in that tiny room, cut off from family,* he thought. The nursing home's strict lockdown policies, meant to protect their vulnerable residents, had also left many feeling trapped and forgotten.

Alex's heart ached as he pictured his mother sitting by her window, watching the world go by. *The isolation must be taking a toll,* he thought, having seen the same on too many EMT calls to seniors with diminished mental and emotional well-being.

The guilt gnawed at him, a nagging reminder that his own loneliness paled in comparison to what his mother must be experiencing. He wished there was more he could do to bridge the gap, to let her know that she was loved and not alone.

I'll call the nursing home first thing tomorrow, Alex thought as he walked the few blocks back to his apartment. Even if he couldn't visit his mother in person, he could at least hear her voice and offer some words of comfort and reassurance.

With a heavy heart, Alex stepped back into his building, the weight of his guilt eclipsing the lingering warmth of the evening's companionship. In this world of isolation and uncertainty, he knew that finding ways to connect with and support loved ones would be more important than ever.

I've got to do better, to be more present for Mom and everyone. The pandemic had taken so much from so many, but it could not take away the love and compassion that bound them together, even across the widest of distances.

For months, Alex had struggled to maintain a sense of normalcy despite the decaying world around him. His job kept him going, though his longing for connection threatened to crack his stoic facade. But he soldiered on, trying to shut out the darkness creeping in from all sides.

Chapter 2: A New Day

The next morning, blaring car horns jolted Alex awake. He groaned and pulled the pillow over his head, trying to tune out the cacophony of sounds that began each day in the Bronx—the rumbling subways, wailing sirens, neighbors shouting. Those urban rhythms formed the musical score of his life.

After a few more minutes of futile avoidance, Alex dragged himself out of bed, the weight of exhaustion heavy on his shoulders. He surveyed his one-bedroom apartment, the modest space he called home in the heart of the Bronx.

The apartment was rent-controlled, a precious commodity in a city where affordable housing was increasingly scarce. It had been under Alex's mother's name for decades, passed down to him when he moved her into the nursing home. The stability of the rent-controlled lease was a blessing, allowing Alex to continue living in the neighborhood he loved on his meager EMT salary.

The living room was small but cozy, with a well-worn greige couch that had seen better days and a scarred coffee table cluttered with medical textbooks and old family photos. A tiny kitchen overlooked the living room, separated by a half-wall that served as a makeshift dining area.

Down a short hallway, Alex's bedroom was just big enough for a double bed and a dresser, with a window that looked out over the bodega. The walls were adorned with posters of Alex's favorite bands and sports teams, remnants of his younger years.

Alex took pride in his apartment despite its age and occasional maintenance issues. It was a piece of his family's history, a connection to the community that had shaped him. The neighbors were like an extended family, always ready with a friendly greeting or a helping hand.

As Alex moved through his morning routine, he reflected on the apartment's many memories—holiday gatherings with his mother, late-night study sessions during his EMT training, and impromptu movie nights with friends. Even in the midst of the pandemic's isolation, the apartment remained a source of comfort and stability.

Stepping into the living room, Alex paused to straighten a framed photo of his mother on the bookshelf. Her warm smile beamed back at him, a reminder of the love and sacrifices that had made this home possible.

Stepping into his tiny bathroom, a quick shower helped Alex shake off his grogginess from the late night at the speakeasy. Drying off with the beach towel Bronx-Lebanon Hospital gave out a couple of years ago for EMS Week, Alex winced slightly at the ache in his right shoulder. That old sports injury had flared up lately, probably from hauling around too many heavy patients.

Back in his bedroom, Alex threw on a pair of loose-fitting, seen-better-days jeans, a hospital T-shirt, and an EMT jacket, the one with a tear in the sleeve. *Good grief, I have got to fix that,* Alex thought for about the tenth time.

He returned to his kitchen, where he shook some painkillers for his shoulder into his palm, then knocked them back with lukewarm coffee he poured from the carafe still in the coffeemaker.

With a deep breath, Alex gathered his mask, gloves, and sanitizer and headed out the door, ready to face another day of serving his community. No matter what challenges lay ahead, he knew that he would always have this little piece of the Bronx to come back to, a place to call his own in a world turned upside down.

The streets of New York showed the first signs of the morning commute. Alex wove between pedestrians hustling to catch their trains and buses. He rode the subway often, when he wasn't on call for emergencies. But today, he was starting a twelve-hour shift, so it was time to get a feel for what was happening across the sprawling city neighborhoods.

Alex met up with his partner, Hassan, at the Bronx-Lebanon Hospital. The former Floridian was just finishing the overnight portion of his own twenty-four-hour shift. Hassan had moved to New York to become a firefighter after receiving an inheritance from his grandmother. However, he found his true calling as an EMT, where his calm demeanor and quick thinking made him an invaluable partner.

Growing up, Hassan had been an avid fan of the Colorado Rockies, a passion he carried with him to the Big Apple. He often wore a faded Rockies cap during their shifts, a reminder of his roots and a conversation starter with patients.

Despite being deeply religious, Hassan kept his faith to himself, never imposing his beliefs on others. His devotion manifested in his unwavering commitment to helping people in need, regardless of their background or circumstances.

As Alex and Hassan headed out to the ambulance for morning rounds, they fell into their familiar rhythm. They had been partners for more than a year, and their complementary skills and personalities made them a well-oiled machine.

Hassan's even-keeled nature balanced out Alex's occasional impulsiveness, while Alex's street smarts and intuition helped Hassan navigate the city's complexities. Together, they faced the daily challenges of the job with a shared sense of purpose and camaraderie.

"How've you been?" Alex asked, smiling reflexively even though it was invisible behind his mask.

"A-OK," Hassan replied. "I went to see my grandmother the other day. I always keep my distance. She's so frail. But I'm so grateful to her that I was able to move here."

"I get you," Alex said, nodding. "If it wasn't for my mom's apartment, I sure couldn't afford to stay here, especially with our hours cut because of this friggin' pandemic. I'm glad I can watch out for the folks on my floor and neighborhood. A lot of them are old and lonely."

Hassan reported that a few minor calls had come in overnight—a kitchen fire, an elderly man with chest pains, and more noteworthy, two drug overdoses. "Had to hit 'em both with Narcan," Hassan said. "This new stuff on the streets is no joke. People are dropping like flies."

Alex nodded as they wrapped up their morning rounds. He'd seen addicts seizing up lately too. The influx of tainted drugs was definitely alarming.

As the morning wore on, Alex and Hassan responded to a series of routine calls—a few minor injuries, a diabetic emergency, and an elderly woman with difficulty breathing. Throughout it all, Hassan's compassion and professionalism shone through, putting patients at ease and ensuring they received the best possible care.

Back in the ambulance after a particularly challenging call, Alex turned to Hassan with a grin. "You know, for a Florida boy, you handle these New York streets like a pro."

Hassan chuckled, adjusting his Rockies cap. "What can I say? I learned from the best. And it doesn't hurt that the traffic is so light right now."

Alex nodded, the unspoken bond between them stronger than ever. As they drove to the next call, he knew that no matter what the day might bring, he could count on Hassan to be right there beside him, a steadfast presence in an uncertain world.

With a shared determination to serve their city, Alex and Hassan continued their shift, a dynamic duo united by their dedication to the job and to each other.

As Hassan drove through the city with Alex in the copilot's seat, they responded to the routine mix of calls—car accidents, a pedestrian hit by a bicyclist, and a convenience store owner suffering heart attack symptoms. It was par for the course on a busy day in the Bronx. Alex almost enjoyed the nonstop pace because it kept his mind from wandering to darker places.

Mid-morning Alex and Hassan stopped at a corner bodega, one of the few shops still open that survived the pandemic. The store's flickering neon OPEN sign invited them in from the deserted streets. Grabbing lukewarm coffees and a few stale donuts had become their daily lunch on the ambulance run.

While Hassan chatted with the weary shopkeeper, Alex took a moment to observe the man behind the counter. He appeared to be in his late fifties, with a thick head of salt-and-pepper hair and a neatly trimmed beard. His weathered face bore the lines of a life spent working long hours, but his dark eyes still held a glimmer of warmth and intelligence.

Alex absent-mindedly skimmed the newspaper headlines by the register. More articles described disturbing attacks plaguing cities abroad.

Experts feared that a mutated virus spawned in remote rainforests was inciting unbridled aggression in people.

Details were scarce, but theories included a mind-altering pathogen or uncontrolled hormone imbalance. The infected people violently lashed out against any living beings, no longer recognizing friend from foe. Footage showed bloodied victims being dragged into the shadows by mobs of hollow-eyed assailants.

As Alex read the troubling reports, unease crept up his spine. *At least that chaos seems confined overseas so far,* he thought.

But Alex knew that New York's dense population made it the perfect breeding ground for *any* pathogen. Still, it was no use panicking prematurely. This was still halfway around the world.

Tossing the paper back on the newsstand, Alex grabbed the coffees and donuts to go, cavalierly brushing the chilling headlines from his mind. Around here, the tainted street drugs caused users to act deranged. That was enough of a crisis to deal with. The papers' reports of a new mind-altering pathogen were likely just more media fear-baiting anyway.

Settling back into the passenger's seat of the ambulance cab, Alex took a long sip of tepid coffee with one hand while fastening his seatbelt with the other. He was ready to respond to the rest of the day's 911 calls, whatever form they took. Everything else was just white noise that had to be blocked out. He had lives to save right here. Headlines on the other side of the world were unnecessary distractions.

As Alex and Hassan navigated the city streets between calls, the ambulance cab became a sanctuary for reflection and conversation. The two partners had developed a comfortable rapport, and their chats helped to alleviate the stress of the job while deepening their understanding of each other.

During a lull in the action, Hassan turned to Alex with a pensive look. "Sometimes I wonder how much longer we can keep this up," he confided, gesturing to the city outside the windshield. "The overdoses, mental health crises, violence—it feels like it's getting worse every day."

Alex nodded, his eyes fixed on the road ahead. "I know what you mean. It's like we're putting out fires left and right, while the root causes smolder beneath the surface."

Hassan leaned back in his seat. With his voice tinged with frustration, he said, "And now, with this pandemic, it's like all the cracks in the system have been exposed—the inequality, the lack of resources, the way society leaves certain people behind."

Alex glanced over at his partner, appreciating the depth of his insight. "You're right. It's not just about treating the symptoms anymore. We need to find ways to address the underlying issues, to give people the support they need *before* they reach their breaking point."

As the pair delved deeper into the conversation, sharing their experiences and perspectives, Alex felt a renewed sense of purpose. These ambulance cab chats weren't just a way to pass the time; they were a chance to grapple with the complex realities of their work and to imagine a better future for the communities they served.

The rest of the day proceeded fairly routinely, with a steady stream of calls that kept them on their toes. They responded to several overdoses, administering Narcan and providing lifesaving care to people in the throes of addiction. They also encountered a number of mental health crises, using their training in de-escalation and empathy to help people in distress.

Interspersed with those more serious calls were a variety of non-life-threatening injuries, including a sprained ankle from a pickup basketball game, a minor kitchen knife cut, and a child with a high fever. Alex and Hassan treated each case with the same level of professionalism and compassion, offering comfort and reassurance to the patients and their loved ones.

As the afternoon wore on, Alex could feel the energy of the city starting to shift. The lengthening shadows and the cooler breeze signaled the approach of evening, and with it, the inevitable uptick in emergencies.

But for now, the chaos was manageable, and Alex welcomed the brief respite before the storm. He knew that the night ahead would likely bring new challenges and heart-wrenching scenes, but he also knew that he and Hassan would face them together, drawing strength from their partnership and their shared commitment to the work.

As they drove on, the ambulance cab chats continued, a lifeline of connection and understanding amidst the turbulence of the city. In these moments of reflection and camaraderie, Alex found the resilience and hope he needed to keep pushing forward, one call at a time.

When their grueling ambulance shift finally ended, Hassan drove home for some needed rest, and Alex caught the train to his weekly physical therapy appointment to treat his aching shoulder. He looked forward to seeing Theresa, his usual therapist, who had become part of Alex's work family after years of appointments.

But as Alex entered the exam room, he was greeted by an unfamiliar face. Instead of his usual therapist, he saw a young woman who appeared to be in her mid-twenties. She had a friendly smile and an air of eager professionalism about her.

Amanda, as she introduced herself, had a petite frame and stood at about 5 feet 4 inches. Her chestnut hair was pulled back into a neat ponytail, revealing youthful features and bright, inquisitive eyes. She wore a set of light blue scrubs, the standard uniform for the clinic's staff, with a name tag that read "Amanda Nichols, PT Trainee."

Alex introduced himself politely, but he felt disappointed. Warmth didn't exactly exude off Amanda. Already, Alex knew he would miss Theresa's warm bedside manner and lighthearted banter if his PT was with Amanda. Amanda was diligent but all business, putting Alex through rigorous exercises to assess his shoulder's range of motion.

"C'mon," Amanda urged, manhandling Alex's shoulder far too much for his liking. Her intense prodding made Alex wince.

"I promise you; I'm barely applying pressure," Amanda said brusquely.

"I'm not sure you understand how much worse the pain is getting," Alex protested. "My shoulder is getting weaker by the day. Lifting my gear and patients keeps getting harder and harder."

"Uh-huh," Amanda absentmindedly grunted, acknowledging Alex's words, all the while jotting messy notes.

This one's no Theresa, Alex thought ruefully.

After a long, awkward silence while Amanda reviewed his chart, Alex was relieved to see Theresa finally arrive. He drew the first full breath he'd taken since he'd arrived.

"Hi Alex, Amanda," Theresa greeted them, her calm presence softening Amanda's clinical roughness. "Amanda will be shadowing me for a few weeks before taking on full patient loads."

Alex smiled to himself, predicting he'd come to see Amanda as "bad cop" alongside Theresa's compassionate, thoughtful "good cop" approach.

"I know you've probably already updated Amanda, but please catch me up," Theresa said. True to form, Theresa listened intently as Alex summarized his symptoms. Then Theresa began realigning exercises to target the affected muscles.

"We'll strengthen you up again real soon," Theresa said before sending Alex on his way with a list of exercises to do at home from Amanda.

As Alex left the therapist's office, he felt the familiar soothed relief that Theresa always gave him. Her gentle manner reminded him of the humanity beneath the clinical visits. He was grateful for her experience guiding his care, especially with the new trainee learning the ropes. Even though today's appointment had been exhausting, it left Alex feeling protected and supported.

Chapter 3: Turning after the Turning Point

A decade ago, by the latter half of 2020, the world was suffering from COVID-19 pandemic fatigue. Endless restrictions strained society's mental health. Illnesses and deaths were still mounting despite precautions. The yearning for a way out was palpable.

Then came the breakthrough: Multiple pharmaceutical teams announced successful vaccine trials, which were developed in record-shattering time thanks to global collaboration. After months of darkness, that news finally brought a ray of light.

As vaccine vials shipped, a collective wave of relief swept across the weary masses worldwide. Frontline medical workers and vulnerable elderly could soon be protected. There was hope of hugging family again, removing masks, and reopening communities.

Even the normally stoic scientific community sounded jubilant. Many scientists were on the verge of tears as they detailed the results of the vaccine trials.

"We have ended this torturous chapter, and our unprecedented efforts will revolutionize medicine!" one researcher exclaimed triumphantly.

Of course, challenges still loomed, notably how to distribute hundreds of millions of doses equitably worldwide. But morale soared with this turning point in sight. Caution remained necessary, but spirits lifted just imagining crowded concerts, sporting events, and family gatherings in the not-so-distant future.

Certainly, no one pretended the grief and scars from the past year would instantly heal. But this remarkable scientific feat promised to lift humanity out of constant crisis toward a chance to recuperate and reconnect again. After so many goodbyes, hope could finally be welcomed back.

Initially, vaccine uptake was high among the general public, which was desperate to return to some semblance of everyday life. Practically overnight, mass vaccination sites popped up to meet demand as people clamored for the shots that could finally liberate them.

In the early months, the news was filled with heartwarming stories and images of grandparents hugging grandkids, masks coming off, restaurants filling up. It appeared the researchers' heroic efforts had paid off handsomely.

But as case numbers dropped substantially, troubling rumors emerged. Whispers circulated about people experiencing bizarre neurological symptoms—or even death—shortly after vaccination. Although the reports were infrequent, they were consistent.

"It's coincidental," some medical experts breezed.

"It's statistically inevitable with hundreds of millions receiving new vaccines," others explained.

In those early months of relief and optimism, the public looked the other way, desperate for normal life to resume.

But victims' families maintained otherwise, pointing to drastic personality shifts, increased aggression, and trancelike behavior in loved ones post-vaccination.

By early 2030, nearly ten years after the initial COVID-19 pandemic lockdowns and mask mandates, the concerned whispers about bad outcomes from vaccines reached critical mass.

Gradually, the dark accounts compounded, and the patterns became too striking to dismiss as chance. The influx of reports could no longer be contained, and fear mutated faster than any virus as questions arose on all sides.

For a fleeting moment, society had dared to hope coming out the other side of its long trial. But old traumas resurfaced to taint even the most valiant victories. The shadows, once held at bay, had only grown longer in wait. Their menace now magnified in a world so weary of battles without end.

Dark theories spread, particularly regarding mRNA technology, which some experts believed might be unexpectedly manipulating brain biology.

Trust in health authorities began deteriorating, especially in certain populations. The erosion of confidence was particularly evident in communities that had historically experienced discrimination or neglect from the medical establishment, such as Blacks, Latinos, and the LGBTQ+ communities.

One emerging pattern was that when people who had already been infected were vaccinated, their risk of these personality shifts and aggression seemed to increase. Fear grew that the cure for COVID-19 might trigger another problem entirely.

As more incidents surfaced, the message became muddled. Were the benefits of the vaccine worth the uncertain side effects? Should people who have recovered get vaccinated at all? Was the cure worse than the disease? Confusion reigned as society's divisions deepened once again.

For a fleeting moment, normalcy had seemed within reach. But ominous questions now lingered. "Could the scientific gold at the end of the pandemic rainbow contain traces of a curse as yet uncomprehended?" asked a particularly vocal anti-vaxxer.

Soon, the media began comparing the victims of post-vaccination "bad outcomes" to zombies, with their trancelike stares, personality changes, and increased aggression.

"Have we entered into the *Night of the Living Dead*?" one national news reporter queried.

At first, the reports of violent, zombie-like post-vaccination reactions were rare. Public health authorities continued to dismiss them as statistically inevitable coincidences. However, as more stories surfaced and the patterns became impossible to ignore, even the scientists were baffled by the biological mechanisms.

Regardless of whether people who had prior COVID-19 infections were treated or had been asymptomatic, they were far more likely to experience extreme neurological reactions than the general vaccinated public who hadn't had COVID-19. These reactions ranged from debilitating migraines and seizures to more alarming conditions such as temporary paralysis, memory loss, and even psychotic episodes. The Centers for Disease Control and Prevention scrambled to determine why. An early theory was that a previous infection could make people susceptible to flipping some switch altered by the vaccines.

"We believe that certain vaccine batches were improperly formulated," some experts claimed.

"It's a conspiracy to exert mind control or permanently modify human DNA," anti-vaccine groups decried.

"We have everything under control," experts from both sides chorused.

But no matter how scientists tried to reassure the public, speculation ran rampant.

As the public's trust deteriorated, vaccine mandates were met with violent unrest from people who feared some invisible switch inside them might flip, making them murderously infected. Public health campaigns pivoted to voluntary participation, but fear was now surging uncontrolled.

As time passed, some of the previously vaccinated people who developed mild cases of these neurological side effects gathered surreptitiously online, sharing stories of being shunned, hunted, even imprisoned. The word being bandied about was "turned." These unfortunates faced discrimination and violence, which forced many of them into hiding. Underground aid networks formed to help hide people who had transformed, who were now hunted for acquiring an infection beyond their control, whose lingering humanity was ignored in the panic.

Not surprisingly, anyone who had been previously vaccinated and then became infected became increasingly shunned from society—even if they showed no neurological symptoms. A dark era of paranoia and tribalism took hold. Daily life became polarized between people who had been vaccinated—the antibody haves (who were now at risk to turn)—and people who had not been vaccinated—the have-nots (who were not at risk to turn).

Prior exposure to COVID-19, regardless of severity, became stigmatized—a scarlet letter marking the tainted. Questions asked of any new acquaintance became fraught with tension. When were you infected? Did you get the before or vaccine after?

Communities implemented antibody screening checkpoints, barring entry to anyone who tested positive for antibodies and therefore might turn. Families cut off relatives; friends turned on friends. Workplaces were segregated, and communities were barricaded. The risk of being near someone who might turn was too immense to ignore.

Scientists worked relentlessly, analyzing genetic data, searching for explanations why previous COVID-19 infections caused some to turn post-vaccination. But the answers remained elusive.

With no solutions at hand, the public's unrest swelled.

Governments struggled to maintain order as protests and riots erupted over the fracturing state of society. The divide had taken hold, pitting citizen against citizen over antibody status. While paranoia remained rampant, trust could not be rebuilt.

Everywhere, the twin pandemics of virus and fear scarred the social fabric, perhaps irrevocably. Healing could not even begin until the biological root cause was uncovered, so scientists toiled endlessly in their labs, racing to discover the mysterious neurological triggers of the disease. Until then, the world hung in limbo, dreading who might next turn.

Chapter 4: An Impossible Escape

Alex spent his few days off relaxing and diligently performing the home exercises that Amanda, his new physical therapist, had prescribed. He found that the exercises helped to alleviate the lingering discomfort in his shoulder, and he appreciated Amanda's attention to detail in creating a personalized rehabilitation plan.

When Alex returned to work, he met up with Hassan at the assignment board, ready to tackle another shift together. With a grin, Alex turned to his partner and said, "Man, it feels like we never left. Time off always goes by way too fast."

Hassan nodded in agreement as his eyes scanned the assignment board. "Tell me about it. I blinked, and suddenly we're back in the thick of it."

As Alex remembered his recent physical therapy session, he rotated his shoulder, testing its range of motion. "Oh, by the way, my shoulder's feeling pretty good. I had a new therapist during my last visit—Amanda. She was thorough, but I call her 'bad cop' because of her no-nonsense approach."

Hassan chuckled, shaking his head in amusement. "You and your nicknames, Alex. You've got one for everyone, don't you?"

The partners' lighthearted banter was interrupted as they both zeroed in on their assignment for the day—their monthly rotation with the SWAT team, which was a duty they had taken on after completing a rigorous tactical combat training course. The specialized training allowed them to work alongside the city's elite tactical unit once a month, providing medical support and assistance in high-risk situations.

"Looks like it's our turn to join the SWAT team today," Alex remarked with a mix of excitement and anticipation in his voice.

Hassan nodded, his expression turning serious. "Yeah, we better gear up and get ready. These rotations always keep us on our toes."

As the pair made their way to the locker room to don their tactical gear, Alex reflected on the intense training they had undergone to qualify for these monthly rotations. The tactical combat course had pushed them to their physical and mental limits, teaching them advanced skills in firearms handling, close-quarters combat, and emergency medical care under fire. *That was intense,* Alex remembered. *Really busted my butt.*

Despite the inherent dangers that came with working alongside the SWAT team, Alex and Hassan took pride in their ability to provide critical medical support in even the most challenging situations. They knew that their presence could mean the difference between life and death for their fellow officers and any civilians caught in the crossfire.

As Alex and Hassan finished gearing up and joined the rest of the SWAT team for their briefing, they exchanged looks of determination and readiness. They knew that their unique combination of medical expertise and tactical training made them valuable assets to the team, and they were prepared to put their skills to the test.

With a final check of their equipment and a nod of acknowledgment to their SWAT team colleagues, Alex and Hassan climbed into the SWAT armored vehicle, ready to face whatever challenges the day might bring. They knew that their monthly rotations with the six-man SWAT team were a testament to their dedication, versatility, and unwavering commitment to serving their community, no matter the risks or obstacles they might encounter along the way.

The first call came in as a routine infected house call—make entry, remove uninfected, exit.

But things quickly went south.

Alex and Hassan entered the home with their respective teams, each via different entries. Practically immediately, Alex's team was overrun by zombies. They were a terrifying sight. These were not the slow, shambling creatures of horror movies past. These undead were fast, agile, and relentless in their pursuit of human flesh. Their skin was a sickly, mottled gray, stretched taut over their emaciated frames. Their eyes, once windows to the soul, were now dim and lifeless, yet somehow still burning with an insatiable hunger.

Desperate to avoid the quick-footed zombies right on his heels, Alex dashed into the home's generously sized laundry room, slamming the door shut behind him. He ducked behind a utility sink in the corner farthest from the door. He could hear the zombies in the hallway, pounding and clawing at the door, eager to feast on him.

The first zombie ripped open the door. Braced for the end, Alex watched it stagger into the laundry room. But then Alex was shocked when it suddenly recoiled, writhing as if repelled by an invisible force. As Alex watched from the far corner of the room, the zombie grasped its head, moaning, before stumbling away.

Right behind, two more zombies burst into the laundry room, then exhibited the same pained, bewildering reactions. They staggered aimlessly about, seemingly unable to detect Alex crouched behind the utility sink right in front of them.

Alex didn't wait for any more zombies to make their way into the laundry room. Seizing the bizarre opportunity, Alex stood, then slipped unharmed past the dazed zombies. He ran down the hall, through the living room, and back outside the front door, where he found what was left of two SWAT team members whose bodies had been decimated by the violent horde.

"I can't be the only one who made it out of there," Alex mumbled, his voice trembling with a mix of abject fear and desperate hope. "Where's Hassan? Please, let him and the others have survived that nightmare."

Alex ran to the command center, where the vehicles had parked a few doors down, with his heart pounding and his mind racing. When he entered the command center, he saw that the rest of his team, thankfully including Hassan, had also managed to make it back, but they were in rough shape. Many of them were covered in cuts, blood, and bruises. Their uniforms were torn and tattered from the intense battle with the zombies.

In stark contrast, Alex appeared relatively unharmed, with only a few minor scratches on his body from ducking behind the utility sink. During the debriefing, the SWAT team leader questioned, "Alex, you look relatively unscathed. How'd you manage that?"

Alex tried to come up with a plausible explanation. "I dunno. Lucky breaks and quick thinking, I guess."

It was evident from the skeptical looks on Alex's teammates' faces that they weren't buying his story. The room was filled with an air of suspicion and disbelief, as if everyone sensed that Alex was holding something back.

"Well, I'm glad that you're okay," the SWAT team leader said with a curt nod of his closely shaved head.

After the debriefing wrapped up and the team prepared to drive back to the station, an uncomfortable silence descended upon them.

As Alex rode in the SWAT vehicle, his mind was a whirlwind of confusion and uncertainty. *Why did those zombies let me be? It doesn't make sense. I should've been a goner.* Alex knew that his experience defied explanation, but he also realized that he couldn't keep it a secret forever.

Back at the station, Alex sought out the chief, knowing that he had to report the unusual incident. With a trembling voice and a heavy heart, Alex explained, "It was the darndest thing, Chief. I can't believe I'm here to tell you about it."

The chief listened intently, his eyes widening with a mix of concern and disbelief. As Alex finished his account, he could see the gears turning in his chief's mind. This was uncharted territory for them both. "I'm just as perplexed as you are, Alex," the chief said, shaking his head. "I'm going to check into this."

Despite the chief's promise to investigate the matter, Alex could tell that he was at a loss for how to proceed. With a sigh, Alex returned to his duties, trying to push the nagging questions and survivor's guilt from his mind. He knew in his gut that this was just the beginning, and that the zombie threat was far from over. But for now, all he could do was focus on his job and try to survive the strange, terrifying new world like everyone else.

After leaving the chief's office more rattled than before, Alex found Hassan waiting for him outside the ambulance. "Let's get back to the bus," Alex said as he and Hassan climbed into the ambulance, each lost in their own thoughts as they tried to process the day's horrific events.

Alex couldn't shake the feeling that his life, and the lives of everyone around him, had been forever changed. The future was uncertain, and he knew that they would all need to rely on each other more than ever before if they hoped to survive the nightmarish horrors that lay ahead.

In the months following that first incident, Alex had several more close calls with the infected that rattled him. When Alex and his team responded to outbreak calls, zombies would often fixate on other team members but leave Alex alone—even when he was the closest to them.

The second time it happened, Alex's heart pounded as the horde chased his teammates while ignoring him just feet away. Even more heartbreakingly, Alex saw the aftermath of some team members who weren't so lucky. They had been ripped to ribbons by the ruthless undead.

What on earth is going on? Alex wondered? *Is it just dumb luck? Or something more?*

After Alex's third bizarre escape, he began to document the occurrences in a note on his phone. He logged the dates, locations, and his proximity to the infected. A pattern emerged: Whenever zombies approached within a couple of meters to Alex, they lost interest, became dazed, and wandered off.

Alex wracked his brain, trying to understand why. What was different about him? The only personal health change he could pinpoint was a recent mild leg tremor. It had become an annoyance, and Alex planned to see a doctor about it soon.

Though it seemed far-fetched, Alex couldn't silence the gut feeling that his tremor might somehow be linked to the zombie immunity. Logically, he knew nothing as hopefully benign as a little twitchy leg should render him invisible to the zombies' detection. Yet the timing made him wonder. *I don't believe in coincidences,* he thought cynically.

Alex hesitated telling anyone else about his close calls with the zombies and his theories, not wanting to sound insane by suggesting a leg tremor could somehow camouflage him from hungry undead. He knew to anyone else it would seem unbelievable. Supposedly, *nothing* could repel these unrelenting infected.

To try to maintain his sanity, Alex continued to methodically document each incident, looking for patterns. His scientifically oriented mind couldn't accept that luck or chance caused the zombies to ignore him repeatedly. His intuition told him that something intervened whenever the undead got close enough to bite. It was like his biology put up an invisible barrier between him and the zombies. Alex became obsessed with understanding why he was immune while others perished around him. Because Alex was suffering from more than a little bit of survivor's guilt, he was desperate to find the underlying reason why.

Alex was determined to stay objective in gathering data, but pattern recognition revealed something significant was happening anytime the ravenous hordes approached within striking distance. An unmistakable stimuli-response occurred that Alex could not rationalize away.

After even more bizarre encounters with the infected, Alex expanded his meticulous documentation, writing down everything he could recall, no matter how small the detail: time of day, weather, exact locations, and proximity to the horde. He believed that someday even minor observations could prove crucial.

Even though Alex was impatient for answers, he forced discipline upon himself. He refrained from irrational theories or confirmation bias because he knew that hard facts and measurable, repeatable steps were essential.

Alex remained open to all hypotheses grounded in science, even those that appeared improbable at first glance. He spent hours googling and going down rabbit holes of research to discover how neurological changes could alter disease pheromones. Obscure East Asian medical journals referenced monasteries where the infected avoided certain meditating monks. Alex exhaustively followed each and every thread.

A few weeks later, during a late-night FaceTime with Hassan, Alex's partner suddenly leaned closer to the screen, squinting at something in the background. "Hey, what's all that stuff on your wall?" he asked, his curiosity piqued.

Alex glanced behind him, realizing that Hassan had caught a glimpse of the sprawling collage of notes, diagrams, and newspaper clippings related to his investigations into the zombie immunity mystery. With a sigh, he turned back to the camera, knowing that it was time to come clean.

"I've been holding out on you, man. I've had more weird interactions with them than I've let on," Alex said, his voice low and serious. "I just don't understand why. Why am *I* being spared when so many other guys have been killed? That's everything I've gathered so far about my strange encounters with the infected," Alex explained, gesturing to the materials behind him. "I just don't understand why. I started tracking every detail, every pattern, every possible clue that could help me understand why they seem to ignore me."

Hassan's eyes widened as he took in the sheer volume of information covering Alex's wall. "I thought something might be up," he said. "You've seemed preoccupied ever since that SWAT mission. You working on this alone?"

Alex nodded, his expression grim. "I know it seems crazy, but I can't shake the feeling that the answer is hidden somewhere in all this data—like a maze that keeps growing, but with a solution waiting at its end." Alex pointed to a particularly complex diagram, connecting various threads of information with colored string. "I've been analyzing everything from the locations and times of the encounters to the environmental factors and my own physiological responses. There has to be a pattern, a reason why I'm different."

Hassan leaned back in his gaming chair, processing the magnitude of Alex's revelation. "Damn, man. I had no idea you were dealing with all this on top of everything else."

Alex gave a rueful smile. "I didn't want to drag anyone else into it until I had something concrete. But I can't do it alone anymore. I need your help, Hassan. I'm burned out."

Hassan nodded, his expression determined. "You know I've got your back, Alex. We'll get to the bottom of this, no matter what it takes."

As the FaceTime ended, Alex felt a weight lift from his shoulders. He was no longer carrying his burden alone, and with Hassan's support, he knew that he could find the answer. The maze might be vast and complex, but together, Alex knew they could navigate its twists and turns until the truth would be finally revealed.

I know the underlying cause will reveal itself in time, Alex thought. *Then this will all make sense logically, however improbably.*

Too many lives hung in the balance not to follow this mystery to its source. Alex vowed never to give up until this scientific truth was uncovered—even if it took years.

Chapter 5: Trembling EMT

Months passed and the city suffered under the dog days of summer without any major incidents involving the infected in the metropolis. The city settled into an uneasy routine, with people adapting to the new normal of constant vigilance and heightened security measures. The occasional skirmish with zombies still occurred, but they were isolated and quickly contained by the authorities.

For Alex and Hassan, life as EMTs continued, albeit with extra preparations and added layers of caution. They responded to calls, treated patients, and worked closely with other first responders to keep the city's citizens safe. However, the specter of the zombie threat loomed over every interaction and every decision made in the field.

After one particularly grueling shift, Alex wanted nothing more than to pick up takeout on his way home to decompress. But as he walked block after block from the station back to his apartment, exhaustion seeped into his bones. By the time Alex reached his apartment building, he was too hot and far too tired to even call for takeout.

I'm sure I have ramen I can cook, Alex thought.

When Alex entered his building, he spotted an "Out of Order" sign on the elevator. He felt blessed that his apartment was on the first floor. Yet, despite being on the first floor, the walk to his door still seemed daunting. Finally, at his door, the promise of collapsing entirely outweighed his hunger. Alex unlocked his door, went inside, and mustered up the energy to lock the door behind him. Kicking off his shoes, he went straight for the fridge and a beer.

As Alex reached to grab a chilled brown bottle, he noticed his left leg trembling again. Looking down, he was relieved that it stopped, as if his leg shook only when he wasn't paying attention to it.

Wow, I must really be tired, Alex thought, then half turned to lean back against the kitchen counter, twisted off the bottle cap, and took a long swig of beer. *This tiredness has gone on too long to be just a bug.* He fought to ignore the fact that his leg had begun trembling again.

Reflecting back on the sheer number of cups of coffee he'd had that day, Alex thought, *Maybe the exhaustion combined with all that caffeine has my nervous system running amok.*

Still leaning against the counter, Alex hurriedly downed the rest of his beer, then a second bottle, hoping alcohol might quiet his racing mind. As the third beer anesthetized the stress of the day, Alex realized how much he had come to rely on drinking to unwind.

By now the trembling in his leg was less noticeable, drowned out by the dizzy haze of alcohol. But deep down, Alex knew his issues couldn't be solely chalked up to the contradictory brew of exhaustion and coffee. After all, he'd been plenty tired before. And he was no stranger to caffeine. The symptoms had been ratcheting up a little bit each day for the past few weeks. Thinking through the implications felt too heavy to face tonight, so Alex stumbled to his bedroom and collapsed into bed fully clothed. The city sounds outside his window soon faded away as he surrendered to sleep.

Over the next few weeks, Alex kept trying to brush off the slight tremor in his left leg as fatigue or stress. As an EMT racing from crisis to crisis, high adrenaline and little sleep came with the territory. But as the weeks passed, the tremors persisted and even intensified. Alex became hyper aware of the involuntary quivering in his leg, which was subtle much of the time, but more noticeable when he was sitting idle or lifting objects.

Oddly, as Alex had noticed before, whenever he purposefully looked down to observe his leg, the shaking would stop, only to return when he glanced away. It was like a flickering switch beyond his control.

The tremors came at inopportune times, such as when Alex was standing for long periods on a scene, sitting in the passenger's seat of the ambulance, or walking up stairs. Any motor task seemed to be a potential trigger.

He cut back on caffeine, still thinking it could be exacerbating things, but the tremors continued. He tried consciously relaxing his muscles and gently massaging his legs to ease tension. But nothing alleviated the quakes.

Colleagues began casting sideways glances when Alex's leg involuntarily shuddered during briefings or patient assessments.

"I'm fine," Alex played it off. "It's just a pinched nerve."

In truth, Alex felt his body rebelling, refusing to be willed into submission. As stressful as the job could be, his physical vitality had never faltered before. Now suddenly, a treacherous fragility was creeping in.

But Alex pushed the worries aside, stubbornly ignoring the signs. If he stopped to confront what this might mean, it would make every creaking stair and spilling mug too real. He willed himself to keep moving forward steadily, at least for now.

Then one morning, Alex was jolted awake by a nightmare of his *right* leg shaking uncontrollably while he was trying to brake an ambulance swerving out of control. Catching his breath, Alex stared down at his legs, which were still under the sheets. Everything seemed fine, but the worry brought on by the all-too-vivid dream lingered.

In the light of a new day, Alex couldn't avoid it any longer. *What is wrong?* he wondered as the exhaustion, what he had come to recognize as tremors, and now vivid dreams prompted his deepest worries. Lying in bed in the morning light, Alex let the reality wash over him. Whatever this was, it had to be faced. The time for avoiding truths and numbing fears was over.

If I don't puzzle this out soon, the tremors might only be the beginning of what I'll lose control of, he thought.

A few nights later at the station, Hassan noticed Alex's leg trembling as he stood and poured them coffee. "Hey, man. Everything okay?" Hassan asked with a raised eyebrow.

Alex nodded and carried the mugs to the table. He sat down quickly as he sipped his coffee, hoping Hassan wouldn't pry further.

Approximately three months after Alex first noticed the tremors in his leg, he began to experience involuntary quivering even when he was performing basic medical tasks. And the quivers were no longer limited to his left leg. One day as he treated a cyclist who had been struck by a car, Alex's unsteady hands trembled as he tried to clean and dress the man's badly scraped body. Fresh blood on Alex's latex gloves amplified the shakiness, making it obvious to the already traumatized patient.

The man eyed Alex warily, his suspicion rising. "Hey, doc, you okay? Your hands are shaking," he said bluntly.

Alex froze momentarily before giving a quick nod and continuing to dress the wounds, avoiding eye contact. Inside, his heart pounded with embarrassment and fear of being reported. But the man simply stared at Alex's trembling gloves as he pressed gauze against torn skin.

In the ambulance, an uncomfortable silence hung between them. Alex kept his head down, intensely self-conscious about his lack of control. He could feel the cyclist's gaze still fixed on his quivering fingers, probably wondering if this visibly unstable EMT could provide proper care.

For the love of God, I'm an experienced, competent EMT, Alex thought, frustration mounting. *Why do I feel so inadequate?*

Despite his mind swirling with thoughts, Alex remained silent. He willed the ambulance to transport the patient to the hospital quickly and his hands to work as steadily as his shaking allowed.

Alex knew the clock was ticking before other people noticed the tremors too. He could cover up and explain away the symptoms for only so long while performing his duties. However unfair it felt, Alex knew soon he would need to come to terms with how his tremors could impact the career he loved if he wanted to help people safely.

But that day in the ambulance, Alex could only take a deep breath and focus on the ambulance ride, willing his hands to be still.

***

Later that week, at Alex's physical training session, Theresa noticed his tremor's persistence.

"Any head injuries lately?" Theresa asked. "This seems neurological."

"Nah, I'm fine," Alex said. "It's just too much caffeine and stress and too little sleep."

Theresa smiled, but Alex thought he detected a whiff of pity in her eyes.

Driving home after this session, more doubts crept in. Alex no longer believed it was just fatigue or caffeine causing his symptoms. *This is starting to feel like something more motor,* he thought. He reflected back to his medical training, and textbook lists of symptoms flashed through his mind. When he arrived back at his apartment, he sat on the edge of his bed and did an assessment.

What are my signs and symptoms? Tremor at rest in hand and foot? Check.

Does anything make it better or worse?

Nothing made it better, but Alex remembered that stressful situations made it worse.

Stooped, shuffling gait? Check.

Alex knew where this pointed, though it terrified him to accept.

Sitting alone in the dark, sirens blaring outside, Alex allowed himself to utter the word: Parkinson's.

It was a disease he witnessed drain his grandmother's once-vibrant life.

He shook his head angrily.

No way. Not that. Not on top of everything else descending into chaos outside these walls.

After an all-too-brief period of calm, the news reports had again grown more alarming, predicting societal collapse if the viral outbreak wasn't contained. Rumors flew that the virus didn't just cause aggression. Those infected lost all humanity, driven only by predatory hunger and violence, like the zombies from the old B-horror movies Alex used to scoff at.

He felt completely overwhelmed, feeling he was simultaneously losing control of his body inside and the safety of his world outside. He laboriously shifted his weight to lie down in bed and fell into a fitful sleep.

Chapter 6: Diagnosis and Discovery

A few days later, alone at night with only his racing thoughts, Alex stared down at his right hand, which was once again trembling against his will. He tightly curled it into a fist, as if sheer force could restrain the involuntary shakes.

In the silence, an unthinkable idea crept unbidden into Alex's mind: *Could these tremors actually be Parkinson's or are they linked to the virus? Is it a coincidence their timing is perfectly aligned?*

Alex's heart pounded as his mind spun hypotheticals. What if this was his body subtly morphing in response to some unseen foreign mutation in the air? What if patient zero had been someone sitting beside him on the subway months back?

The implications were too terrifying to entertain. Alex shook his head, angrily forcing the thoughts away. This was surely just anxiety talking, some irrational doomsday belief arising from the surrounding hysteria.

In Alex's logical mind, he knew a tremor was unlikely to be caused by some unknown virus.

But his darkest instincts nagged at him: *What if?* During this unprecedented time, could any notion be so easily dismissed?

He refused to venture down that rabbit hole any further. He had to maintain focus on his health so he could support his patients. Worrying would only make daily functioning harder, so he silenced the nagging doubts for now. Surely, the shaking was just the first sign of some manageable condition. He decided he would see a doctor soon and get to the bottom of it. Until then, he had to stay strong and keep his world steady amidst the swirling chaos.

Still, as exhaustion overtook Alex, unwelcome theories flashed through his dreamscape. And when he startled awake, heart racing, the hand and leg quivering at his side felt like an ill omen— either of some personal trial ahead or connected to the greater storm brewing outside.

Concerned about the worsening tremors and the constant feeling of exhaustion, Alex finally decided to schedule an appointment with his primary care doctor. He had been putting it off for weeks, hoping that the symptoms would subside on their own, but the incident with the cyclist had been a wake-up call. *I can't hide this for much longer,* Alex thought grimly.

***

The next week at his doctor appointment, Alex sat in the waiting room, his left leg bouncing nervously as he filled out the pre-appointment paperwork.

He tried to focus on the questions about his medical history and current symptoms, but his mind kept wandering back to the moments when his tremors had interfered with his work.

When a nurse called his name, Alex followed her into an examination room with his heart pounding in his chest. He explained his symptoms to the nurse, then repeated them to the doctor. *Why do I have to repeat this when she typed them all up?* Alex wondered, not for the first time. He described the tremors that had started in his left leg, followed by his right, then gradually spread to his hands, as well as the overwhelming fatigue that seemed to follow him like a shadow.

The doctor listened intently, typing notes in Alex's chart as he spoke. "Given your hectic schedule as an EMT, with long shifts and irregular hours, your symptoms are likely a result of exhaustion. Have you heard of fasciculation? That can cause muscle twitches and tremors. It's often associated with stress and fatigue."

Alex listened intently, nodding to show he was keeping up.

"I understand that your job is incredibly demanding, both physically and emotionally," the doctor said, looking up briefly from his laptop screen. "It's not uncommon for EMTs to experience symptoms like these when they're pushed to their limits."

Alex nodded again, feeling a small sense of relief at the doctor's words. Maybe this wasn't as serious as he had feared. Maybe he just needed some rest and a chance to recharge. Alex grabbed onto that glimmer of hope with both hands.

The doctor typed in a prescription for muscle relaxers, then blasted it to the pharmacy that Alex had rarely needed. "That'll be filled for you soon," the doctor said as he smartly shut his laptop. "Take it as directed, and make sure you're getting enough rest when you're off duty. I know that's easier said than done, but it's important to take care of yourself, especially in a job like yours."

"Thanks, doc," Alex said to the doctor's back as he hurried out of the room with his laptop under his arm. Alex gathered his phone and jacket, then left the office. He stopped by the pharmacy on his way home to pick up the prescription, hoping that the muscle relaxers would be the solution he needed to get back to his normal self.

Back home, Alex washed down the pills with sips from a bottle of water.

***

Despite Alex's hope that the medication would be a panacea for his problem, it was anything but.

It wasn't too long before the side effects kicked in. The medication made Alex's shifts a slog. He moved in slow motion, his reactions dulled. One day while Alex was driving the ambulance, Hassan cast him a wary look from the passenger's seat. "Bro, are you drunk?" Hassan asked bluntly. There was no need to mince words between friends.

Alex shook his head, embarrassed, keeping his hands at 10 and 2 on the wheel of the bus. "Oh

God no. It's these muscle relaxers my doc has me on," he explained. "They've got me so drowsy I can barely function."

"No judgment. Just gotta make sure you're safe behind the wheel," Hassan replied. "Maybe you should see about adjusting the meds, though, until you're more functional."

Alex nodded. He knew Hassan was right; he couldn't keep working in this fog. The doctor meant well by prescribing the meds and rest, but clearly, another intervention was needed.

A nagging thought kept circling around in Alex's brain, like wiggling worms: *Could this be Parkinson's?* The niggling thought crescendoed to a scream, so Alex called to ask his primary doctor for a referral to a specialist, hoping to find answers quickly.

Alex called the hospital's scheduling line and learned that the wait to see a neurologist was only a few months; however, Alex was told the nearest movement disorder specialist (MDS) couldn't see him for *eight* months. As an EMT, Alex knew that an MDS was the best choice for accurately diagnosing and treating a condition like Parkinson's disease. These specialists had extensive training and experience in identifying and managing complex neurological disorders that affect movement and coordination.

Alex hung up the phone, feeling a mix of frustration and resignation wash over him. He went to the MDS scheduling site, which confirmed the grim news. The earliest appointment available with an MDS to get any possible understanding of what was happening with his body was eight months away. The news was disheartening, especially given the progressive nature of his symptoms.

The long wait time was a bitter pill to swallow. Eight months felt like an eternity when faced with the daily challenges of uncontrollable tremors and increasing difficulty performing his job. Alex worried about how much worse his symptoms might become in the intervening months and how they could impact his ability to care for his patients.

After weeks of endlessly refreshing the clinic website, hoping for an earlier cancellation, Alex decided to try contacting other neurology practices. But everywhere had extensive waiting lists, with most unable to see new patients for three to six months.

Driven by a growing sense of urgency, Alex decided to take matters into his own hands. He contacted his insurance company, meticulously noting every in-network neurological clinic within a reasonable distance. Armed with that list, he embarked on a determined campaign to secure an earlier appointment.

Alex spent hours on the phone, with his EMT shift radio silent beside him as he called clinic after clinic. With each call, he carefully explained his situation—the progressive tremors, their impact on his work as an EMT, and the pressing need for timely care. His voice, usually steady in the face of emergencies, carried a hint of desperation as he pleaded his case to receptionists and scheduling coordinators.

"I understand you're booked, but is there any way to get in sooner?" Alex found himself repeating, hoping that persistence might uncover a hidden opening. "Even a short consultation would be helpful. I just need some direction."

Despite numerous rejections and long wait times, Alex refused to give up. He knew that somewhere out there, a neurologist might have an unexpected cancellation or a moment of empathy that could fast-track his diagnosis. As Alex dialed yet another number, he steeled himself for disappointment but clung to the hope that this call might be the one to finally provide a path forward out of the maddening uncertainty that had become his daily reality.

Finally, a receptionist took pity upon Alex and managed to squeeze him into an opening just three months away due to a recent cancellation. Alex felt conflicted—relieved to get in somewhere sooner, but frustrated that three more months of decline were in store before any potential relief of moving forward with whatever was wrong. The not knowing was getting daunting

Still, even a three-month wait was better than the alternative—sitting idle while his health deteriorated without guidance or support. Alex knew that he had to be proactive, given the healthcare system strain. This appointment was progress, however modest.

Over the next weeks, he focused on maintaining normalcy despite his limitations. But the waiting game persisted in the back of his mind, a nagging unease. Patience had never been his strong suit when it came to health issues.

As the weeks passed, Alex tried to maintain a sense of perspective and focus on the things he could control. He knew that dwelling on the uncertainty and the long wait for answers would only lead to more stress and anxiety. And he had noticed that only made his symptoms worse.

Instead, Alex channeled his energy into taking care of himself, both physically and mentally. He made a point to eat well, engage in activities that brought him joy and relaxation, and get plenty of rest—as his primary care doctor had ordered. Whether it was reading a favorite book, watching a beloved movie, or taking a long walk in the park, Alex sought out moments of peace and normalcy amidst the chaos he battled both inside and out-side of his body.

At work, Alex continued to give his all, despite the challenges posed by his symptoms. He leaned on Hassan for support and found ways to adapt his techniques to accommodate his changing abilities. He knew that every day he was able to serve his community was a victory, no matter how small.

Even as Alex focused on the present, he tried to hold on to the hope for the future that his symptoms weren't indicative of a life-threatening condition. He tried to stay optimistic, reminding himself that many treatable conditions could cause tremors and weakness.

But in the quiet moments, when the uncertainty crept back in, Alex found himself turning to his support system for comfort and reassurance. He talked to his close friends, sharing his fears and leaning on their love and encouragement. He even reached out to other EMTs who had faced similar health challenges, finding solace in their shared experiences.

The uncertainty of the recent months had been agonizing for Alex, who had been grappling with a roller coaster of emotions ever since the first tremors appeared in his leg. The initial shock and disbelief had gradually given way to a growing sense of anxiety and helplessness as the symptoms persisted.

Every day brought new challenges and uncertainties. Would his tremors interfere with his ability to perform critical medical procedures? Would his colleagues and superiors notice the changes and question his fitness for duty? Would he be able to continue the job he loved and had dedicated his life to? If not, how on earth would he pay his bills and put food on the table?

The lack of answers and the long wait for a definitive diagnosis compounded Alex's mental and emotional strain. He found himself constantly second-guessing his own body, wondering if each new twitch or moment of fatigue was a sign of something more serious. He hated to admit it to himself, but the tremors were worse and more frequent. He also struggled with weakness, especially on the right side of his body. *Why'd it have to be my right side?* he wondered as he found it increasingly difficult to write with his right hand, maneuver a cup of coffee to his mouth, and even navigate the gas and brake pedals in the ambulance.

The agonizing uncertainty made it difficult for Alex to plan for the future or find peace in the present. He felt like he was in a state of constant limbo, unable to move forward or fully come to terms with his situation until he had a clear understanding of what he was dealing with.

Despite Alex's best efforts to stay positive and focused on his work, the weight of the unknown hung heavy on his shoulders. He found himself lying awake at night, his mind racing with worst-case scenarios and unanswered questions.

Even in moments of relative calm, the specter of uncertainty was always lurking in the background, ready to resurface at the slightest provocation. It was a constant companion, an unwelcome presence that Alex couldn't seem to shake no matter how hard he tried.

As the months dragged on, he began to feel a sense of desperation creeping in. He needed answers. He needed to know what he was up against and how he could fight back. The waiting game was taking its toll, and he knew that he couldn't continue to live in this state of agonizing uncertainty.

Chapter 7: The Moment of Truth

Finally the day of Alex's MDS appointment arrived on a frigid, late-January day. He sat anxiously on a cushioned chair in the exam room, purposely avoiding the white paper–covered patient exam table.

After an excruciatingly long wait, Alex heard the doctor tapping the door open with his knuckles and watched him rush in, while introducing himself, "Alex, hello. I'm Dr. Kapoor." The MDS swung the room's only stool around to position it behind the laptop desk on a moveable arm, then plopped his fit body on it, legs spread to steady himself.

With barely a glance at Alex, Dr. Kapoor stared intensely at the laptop screen as his fingers flicked at the mouse pad, scrolling rapidly through what Alex presumed was his electronic medical record.

"I see your maternal grandmother had Parkinson's disease," Dr. Kapoor murmured, mostly to himself, as he continued to scroll. "You are quite young for this to be Parkinson's. But if I was a betting man, I'd bet that it would be Parkinson's."

With that somber news delivered, Dr. Kapoor shifted his gaze to peer over the top of the laptop at Alex seated just a few feet away in the tiny exam room.

By that point, Alex was desperate for *any* diagnosis, *any* relief from the paralyzing uncertainty. So he nodded eagerly, hoping for answers.

But the doctor held up a hand. "Let's not jump to conclusions just yet though. We need to rule out other potential causes properly first."

"Other causes?" Alex asked, feeling a smidge of self-satisfaction that he might have honed on his diagnosis correctly months ago. "Like what?"

"Well, conditions such as stroke, brain lesions, or nerve damage can sometimes present with similar symptoms to yours, including tremors and weakness on one side of the body," Dr. Kapoor said. "We'll need to do a full neurological workup to get a clearer picture of what's going on."

"What does that involve?" Alex asked, though he had a bit of an idea from all of the googling he had been doing during the long wait for this appointment.

"We'll start with an MRI and a CT scan of your brain. Those imaging tests will allow us to look for any structural abnormalities or signs of damage that could be causing your symptoms," Dr. Kapoor said, his voice void of emotion.

"Okay, that makes sense," Alex said, beginning to tire of his constant nodding. "What else?"

"In addition to the scans, we'll run a series of analyses to assess your nerve function and check for any signs of neuropathy or other issues that could be contributing to your tremors and right-side weakness," the doctor answered.

"So, basically, you're going to be looking at my brain and nerves from every angle to see if there's anything else that could be causing these problems?" Alex asked.

"Exactly. We want to be thorough and rule out all other possibilities before we make a Parkinson's diagnosis," Dr. Kapoor said, allowing a bit of compassion to creep into his voice. Without pausing to allow Alex to respond, he continued, "In the past, we had to rely on observation of symptoms and response to medications like carbidopa-levodopa to confirm Parkinson's. That's likely how your grandmother was diagnosed.

"But today we have more definitive diagnostic tools," the doctor went on. "I recommend you get a DaTscan. That's a test that measures the absorption rate of a radiological dye. Depending upon that absorption rate, it confirms the lack of dopamine in the brain along with the diagnosis of Parkinson's disease. The scan can support the diagnosis of young-onset Parkinson's."

Alex nodded again, grateful for how far technology had come. He wondered if this technology had been available decades before when his grandmother developed symptoms, would she have been diagnosed earlier? How different would her outcome have been? He was glad modern medicine could offer more concrete answers about the road ahead for him.

Still, Alex left the appointment frustrated, with more questions than answers. He hated feeling in limbo. But even the prospect of a Parkinson's diagnosis felt better than the uncertainty that had been eating away at him daily.

Over the next few weeks, Alex underwent the ordered MRI, CT scan, and analyses. With each test that came back negative, Parkinson's disease became the more and more likely culprit. Alex began to prepare himself for the diagnosis, steeling himself against the ramifications of having a lifelong, debilitating disease. But without having a concrete diagnosis, Alex clung to fragile hope that it could still be something else.

First thing one Monday morning, Alex's phone rang.

"All of your previous tests were negative," explained the freakishly cheerful physician's assistant on the other line. "Doctor Kapoor wants to order that DaTscan now. A dopamine transporter scan is a noninvasive imaging test that can help diagnose Parkinson's disease and other Parkinsonian syndromes. It involves injecting a radioactive tracer that emits gamma rays, which are then detected by a special camera."

"Will they also put me on Parkinson's meds?" Alex asked, remembering that when his grandmother had been diagnosed, she had been prescribed Parkinson's medication to see if her symptoms improved.

"No, we don't do that anymore," the physician's assistant replied. "The DaTscan is confirmation enough."

"Okay," Alex consented to the exam, which the physician's assistant quickly scheduled for two weeks later.

***

The Friday before Alex's DaTscan, he received a call from the radiology department. "Have you received authorization from your insurance company?" the radiation nurse asked.

Confused, Alex called his insurance company and learned that his insurance had denied coverage for the $50,000 test.

"Don't attend that appointment to avoid being charged," the insurance company's rep advised gravely.

Alex contacted the doctor's office, which promised to fight the insurance company's decision. Two months passed before Alex received an email stating that an independent auditor had made the final decision: The insurance would not cover the exam.

Immediately, Alex called his doctor. "What are my options?" he asked.

After a painfully long pause, the doctor explained, "You could either deal with the tremors or start taking medication."

Alex hung up the phone, perplexed and frustrated. He didn't want the quick fix of trying the medication without seeing an expert for a conclusive diagnosis.

Fortunately, Alex had not canceled his original appointment with the neurologist—a Dr. James in a nearby borough. However, she was out on maternity leave, forcing Alex to reschedule for four months later, after her return to the practice, in February 2031. Despite the setbacks, Alex remained determined to get a proper diagnosis.

Two weeks after Alex's fortieth birthday, he finally saw Dr. James. After a brief examination lasting only five to ten minutes, Dr. James performed what Alex later learned is called a Unified Parkinson's Disease Rating Scale, a strange ceremony-like physical exam of tapping Alex's hands and feet and pushing him back and forth—which to Alex felt like a woefully antiquated, inadequate test, especially considering it took more than a year to get it yet it seemed to carry as much weight as the denied $50,000 DaTscan.

Following the tapping and the pushing maneuvers, Dr. James sat back in her seat, took a deep breath, looked at Alex, and delivered the diagnosis.

"You have Parkinson's disease."

The certainty of the diagnosis hit Alex like a blow. It felt like all of the air had been sucked out of the room, leaving him feeling breathless and winded. Like a rush of air filling the void, Alex felt a moment of relief. Finally, the racing in his mind quieted. He finally had an answer—though it was far from the one he wanted.

And truth be told, it was far from the answer he *expected,* after so many months of uncertainty and buildup. Alex felt a mix of relief at finally having an answer and apprehension about what lay ahead. He knew that while one journey had ended, another was just beginning. With the diagnosis confirmed, Alex was ready to start treatment and move forward, facing the challenges of living with Parkinson's head-on.

"I recommend we try this medicine," Dr. James said, tapping the notes into her laptop. "On your way out, schedule a one-month follow-up."

Feeling summarily dismissed, Alex stumbled out of the neurologist's office in a daze, with the Parkinson's disease diagnosis still ringing in his ears. He stepped outside into the bright sunlight, emotions swirling, then somehow managed to put one foot in front of the other to cross the parking lot to his F150.

Alex sat motionless in his parked truck for nearly an hour, emotionally stunned as his entire envisioned future collapsed and reconfigured before his eyes.

Finally, Alex put his key in the ignition, rolled down the driver's and passenger's side windows, put the car into drive, and began driving on auto-pilot without a conscious destination. Moving felt better than sitting with his spiraling thoughts. He needed to clear the mental fog somehow.

Miles passed aimlessly, the road unfolding ahead through a tunnel-vision haze. Briefly, Alex considered returning to his apartment to process it all. But the four walls of his place seemed confining, almost taunting.

The breeze rolling through the open windows eased Alex's nerves slightly. Clarity came with the white noise of momentum; avoiding this new reality would only magnify the suffering. Alex's hands firmly gripped the wheel as he readied himself for the uncertainties ahead.

Glancing in the rearview mirror, Alex glimpsed his pale reflection, a shadow of the man who had strolled confidently into the neurologist's office hours ago. But something more profound than appearance had shifted. Alex knew that he would never be his old self again.

As his brain slowly came back online, he switched on the truck radio, trying to regain some normalcy. In the radio's low drone, he caught words about the virus reaching global pandemic levels. Alex's eyes reflexively shot to the stubborn tremor in his right hand, still quivering atop the steering wheel.

Of course it was absurd to think a degenerative disease somehow heralded this catastrophe. It was just a morbid coincidence. But to Alex, the world felt full of unseen connections and ruptures. Few things felt definite in this new life unfolding.

Alex continued to drive, destination uncertain. As the first tears escaped his eyes, he bowed his head, letting the grief wash over him. Today marked the dividing line between Before and After. But bit by bit, the light would return. With his right hand trembling but his resolve firm, Alex drove onward into unfamiliar territory, transformed but undaunted.

***

A couple of days later back at work, Alex sat in the ambulance beside Hassan, working up the nerve to tell him about the diagnosis.

Alex felt a brief reprieve when the dispatch radio crackled to life, its urgent tones cutting through the ambient noise of the bus. Alex and Hassan exchanged knowing glances as a familiar address echoed through the speakers. It was a location they had visited numerous times before, and the familiarity brought with it a mix of concern and determination.

"Looks like we're headed back to Mrs. Rodriguez's place," Hassan said, already reaching for the ignition.

Alex nodded, his mind racing through the possible scenarios they might encounter at the old lady's abode. "Yeah. I hope she's okay. Last time we were there, her condition seemed to be deteriorating."

As Hassan pulled the ambulance out into traffic, lights flashing and siren wailing, Alex reflected on the many calls they had answered at that address. Each visit seemed to reveal another layer of Mrs. Rodriguez's complex medical history. *I feel her struggle,* he thought.

The familiar route unfolded before them as they navigated the city streets, both EMTs mentally preparing for whatever challenges awaited them at their destination. Moments like these reminded Alex why he had chosen this profession—the opportunity to make a difference in people's lives, even if it meant returning to the same life over and over.

Hassan skillfully navigated the busy streets, then pulled up in front of the address and double-parked the vehicle. Alex and Hassan grabbed the stretcher and wheeled it up to the front door. Before they had the chance to ring the bell, the door was opened by a middle-aged blonde home health aide.

Once inside the homey but overly warm front room, Alex saw the elderly Mrs. Rodriguez sitting on her sofa, hands clasped in her lap and shaking. Looking at her reminded Alex of his grandma's Parkinson's disease symptoms—the tremors and fidgeting. Standing next to the sofa in the shadow of the darkened room stood a young man who Alex assumed was Mrs. Rodriguez's son.

Hassan entered the room right behind Alex, with his equipment bag in his left hand. With his right hand, he gestured to Mrs. Rodriguez, silently requesting permission to sit next to her on the couch. The elderly lady nodded in affirmation.

Meanwhile, Alex pulled the only chair in the room up closer to face the couch. The home health aide lingered in the doorway, anxiously shifting her weight from side to side.

As Hassan expertly checked Mrs. Rodriguez's blood pressure and heart rate, Alex queried the aide, pen and pad at the ready to jot down notes. "What prompted you to call us today?" he asked.

The aide's gaze flicked over to the quaking Mrs. Rodriguez, then she said, "She can't seem to sit still. Last night she was all blocked up. Constipated."

"What medications is she taking?" he asked.

"She's taking carbidopa-levodopa," the aide reported.

Alex recognized the Parkinson's disease medication and said, "Oh! She has Parkinson's."

"No she doesn't," the aide replied abruptly.

Alex looked at the aide quizzically without saying a word. He knew Mrs. Rodriguez's symptoms were consistent with the disease and side effects of the medication, such as dystonia and constipation. But he chose to say nothing to the aide. Instead he turned to Hassan and said, "Let's load her up."

After Alex and Hassan loaded the woman into the ambulance and turned to get into the bus, her son, who had followed the gurney out of the house, gestured to Alex that he needed to say something.

"My mom recently received a Parkinson's disease diagnosis," he said in a low voice.

"Thank you for letting me know," Alex said quietly. Although he had suspected as much, he was stunned by the coincidence, having just learned of his own diagnosis.

Hassan hopped into the driver's seat and started the engine. Alex nodded to the son and got into the back of the ambulance with Mrs. Rodriguez. After efficiently checking Mrs. Rodriguez's vital signs and confirming that she was safely secured, Alex opened up to the woman about his new diagnosis and family history with Parkinson's.

"I wouldn't usually talk about myself with a patient, but I was recently diagnosed with Parkinson's," Alex said. "My grandmother had it too. It was rough."

The old woman patted Alex's hand gently. "This is *your* Parkinson's, not your grandmother's," she said wisely.

When they reached the hospital, Alex felt an immense sense of relief having confided in someone. He and Hassan expeditiously released Mrs. Rodriguez from the ambulance, then wheeled her into the emergency department. Hassan left as quickly as they had come, while Alex remained to brief the hospital nurse.

Then Alex walked back out to Hassan, who was waiting by the ambulance, holding a Styrofoam cup of coffee in his hand.

"You okay?" Hassan asked, with concern lacing his words. "You looked upset earlier."

Alex took a deep breath. "Actually there's something I need to tell you ..."

"What's up, man?" Hassan asked, the concern in his voice ratcheted up a notch.

Alex took another breath. "So, you know how I've been struggling with some shakiness and coordination issues lately? I finally went to a neurologist." He paused, unsure how to break the news gently. "Turns out I have Parkinson's disease. Still early stages, but that's why I've been off my game."

Hassan turned to look more directly at Alex, setting down his coffee on the curb next to the ambulance. "Oh damn, bro. I'm so sorry to hear that." He put a hand on Alex's shoulder. "How are you holding up?"

"Honestly, it's been rough coming to terms with it all," Alex sighed. "But I'm trying to take it one day at a time."

"Thanks for telling me," Hassan said. "I could tell something was up with you. I'm sorry to hear this is what it is though. Let me know if there's any adjustments I can make to help you out. And if you ever need to talk, I'm here. Don't worry; your secret's safe with me."

Alex nodded gratefully. It felt good to have told Hassan and to hear his partner understand what he was facing. "Thanks, I'll definitely take you up on that. For now though, I think I'm going to be okay."

Just then, the radio cracked to life with a new emergency. Hassan smiled and gestured to it. "What do you say? Ready to go save some lives?"

"Absolutely," Alex replied, smiling. He turned on the siren as he pulled the ambulance out into the street. With his partner's support, he felt ready to fight this disease while continuing to do what he loved.

Although Alex's fear of judgment lingered, he also felt lighter. No matter the diagnosis, he knew he could still make a difference for patients like Mrs. Rodriguez. And with Hassan's support, he knew he was ready to face this fight.

After the long, busy shift and finally feeling a little unburdened, back at his apartment later that night, Alex dove into Parkinson's research, determined to understand this new enemy facing him. He read information from Parkinson's organizations, explored popular health sites, and even studied scientific articles. He joined several Parkinson's online support groups. Alex voraciously consumed all of the information he could find on Parkinson's. *I have to know everything I can to fight this,* he thought.

A few nights later on an obscure online forum, Alex came across a chilling thread started by a person named Sam that described Parkinson's disease patients having close calls with the infected where they were ignored—as if invisible. Many of the posters hypothesized that their neurological chemistry somehow provided camouflage from the infecteds' detection.

Alex's heart raced. Their accounts sounded eerily similar to what *he* had experienced. He desperately replied to the thread, "Has anyone else experienced this phenomenon?"

A few moments later, Alex received a message back from Sam.

Chapter 8: An Analytical Ally

Sam Rhodes, a towering man at 6 feet 4 inches and 260 pounds, cut an imposing figure despite his gentle demeanor. At 46, his once jet-black hair had begun to silver at the temples, giving him a distinguished air that belied his small-town West Virginia roots. His piercing blue eyes, set deep in a face weathered by years of intense concentration, seemed to see through problems rather than merely observe them.

From an early age, Sam's logical, analytical mind set him apart in his rural community. While other children played sports or chased each other through farm fields, young Sam hunched over disassembled radios and clocks in his father's workshop. His large hands moved with surprising grace as he examined each component, mentally cataloging its function and purpose.

Hours would slip by unnoticed as Sam lost himself in the intricate mechanics of everyday objects. His parents often joked that they had to remind him to eat because he was so absorbed in his latest project. This fascination with how things worked extended beyond just gadgets. Sam applied the same meticulous analysis to natural phenomena, social interactions, and later, complex computer systems.

Despite Sam's imposing physical presence, his soft-spoken manner and thoughtful pauses before speaking gave him an air of quiet authority. His childhood in that small West Virginia town had instilled in him a strong work ethic and a down-to-earth approach to problem-solving that served him well as he navigated the high-tech world of IT.

Sam's natural curiosity led him to pursue engineering and computer science at the University of Virginia. He had an uncanny knack for examining systems and understanding what made them tick, and his ability to problem-solve complex technical challenges earned him respect in the field.

Sam's career trajectory was as impressive as it was unexpected for someone from his humble beginnings. Starting as a junior programmer at a small software company in Charleston, West Virginia, Sam quickly distinguished himself with his knack for elegant, efficient code and his ability to see the bigger picture in complex systems.

Sam's reputation for solving seemingly intractable problems spread as he rapidly rose up the ranks. He became known as the go-to guy for troubleshooting database issues, often finding novel solutions that others had overlooked. His ability to translate technical jargon into layman's terms made him popular with both the IT department and upper management.

By Sam's early thirties, he had outgrown his home state, accepting a position with a Fortune 500 company in Chicago. Fortunately, Sam didn't have to relocate to the Windy City because his work was fully remote. Sam thrived in the fast-paced corporate environment, quickly moving from managing small teams to overseeing entire departments. His projects grew in scale and complexity, from streamlining inventory systems for national retail chains to implementing robust cybersecurity measures for international banks.

Sam found a deep sense of satisfaction in optimizing large-scale IT systems. He approached each project like a massive puzzle, identifying inefficiencies and bottlenecks with an almost preternatural intuition. His strategic tweaks often resulted in significant improvements in both efficiency and output, saving his employers millions of dollars and earning him a reputation as a miracle worker in the IT world.

One of Sam's most notable achievements was the complete overhaul of a multinational corporation's global network infrastructure. Over the course of 18 months, he led a team that redesigned and implemented a new system that increased data transfer speeds by 300 percent—while simultaneously reducing operating costs by 25 percent. The project was hailed as a game-changer in the industry, and it cemented Sam's status as a visionary in his field.

Despite Sam's success, he never lost touch with his roots or his passion for hands-on problem-solving. He could often be found in server rooms late at night, personally fine-tuning systems and mentoring younger team members. His down-to-earth approach and genuine enthusiasm for his work inspired loyalty and admiration from his colleagues at all levels and ages.

As Sam approached his mid-forties, he had reached the upper echelons of his profession, serving as the Chief Information Officer for a leading tech company. Yet even as he navigated boardrooms and shareholder meetings, he remained at heart the curious boy from West Virginia, always eager to understand how things worked and how they could be made better.

But years before, in his late thirties, Sam had begun experiencing a subtle symptom of stiffness in his left arm, called dystonia, that his engineering mind couldn't ignore. With meticulous precision, he documented every change, analyzing each new development with an almost academic detachment. His natural inclination to research kicked into high gear as he sought to understand and overcome this new challenge.

Still living in rural West Virginia, Sam faced the additional hurdle of limited access to specialized medical care. Without an MDS nearby, he worked closely with his local neurologist, piecing together the puzzle of his symptoms, which had progressed to include fatigue, restlessness, apathy, and anxiety attacks. After months of tests and consultations, his neurologist reached out to a specialist at the University of Virginia Medical Center, who ultimately ordered a DaTscan.

On Sam's fortieth birthday, he received the official diagnosis: Parkinson's disease. The reality hit him hard, shaking the foundations of his logical worldview. For the first time in Sam's life, he felt his analytical mind failing him, unable to compute a solution to this deeply personal problem. He spiraled for a time, unmoored by the loss of control over his own body and future.

The diagnosis affected every aspect of Sam's life, including his passion for golf. Once a skilled player of near-professional caliber, he now found himself struggling with the most basic aspects of the game. Holding a golf club induced terrible anxiety, while dystonia prevented him from maintaining his once-perfect grip. The mental fog that accompanied his condition left him unable to analyze shots with his former clarity and precision.

For Sam, this loss was about more than just a hobby. Golf had been a sanctuary where his analytical mind could shine, where complex calculations of wind speed, club selection, and body mechanics came together in perfect harmony. Now, standing on the green, he felt like a stranger to himself, his once-reliable body and mind betraying him at every turn.

As Sam grappled with his new reality, he realized that his journey with Parkinson's would require more than just his intellect. It would demand a kind of adaptability and resilience he had never before needed to cultivate. With the same determination that had driven his career, Sam set out to face this new challenge, knowing that while he couldn't cure Parkinson's, he *could* learn to live with it—and perhaps even find new ways to thrive.

But when the zombie outbreak hit, Sam found a strange purpose in researching the intersection between his disease and the epidemic. He leaned into his gifts for data synthesis and deduction, propelled by this new mystery to unravel.

Driven by a sense of scientific duty and his innate curiosity, Sam researched the mysterious link between Parkinson's disease and the apparent zombie immunity it granted. His analytical mind, honed by years of solving complex IT problems, now turned to this unprecedented biological puzzle.

Sam spent countless hours data mining, poring over medical journals, and analyzing patient reports. He sought answers to questions that plagued him:

What specific neurochemical changes in Parkinson's patients made them undetectable to the infected?

Could this immunity be replicated in healthy people—*without* inducing Parkinson's symptoms?

Was there a correlation between the severity of Parkinson's symptoms and the strength of the zombie repellent effect?

Could understanding this phenomenon lead to a cure for Parkinson's or a vaccine against the zombie virus?

Despite Sam's tireless efforts, his progress was frustratingly slow. The complexity of the human brain, combined with the unpredictable nature of the zombie virus, made for a daunting challenge. Sam often found himself hitting dead ends and running into contradictory data.

However, Sam's compassion for fellow Parkinson's patients drove him to persevere. He couldn't shake the image of frightened people and families, desperately seeking hope in a world turned upside down. Sam knew that his analytical skills, if successful, could restore not just hope but a semblance of order to the chaos unfolding around them.

As Sam delved deeper into the research, he found himself increasingly fascinated by the science behind Parkinson's disease. His engineering background gave him a unique perspective on the neurological processes involved. He began to see the brain as an incredibly complex machine, with Parkinson's as a glitch in its operating system—a glitch that, paradoxically, provided protection against an even greater threat.

This fascination helped Sam cope with his own fears about the disease. By approaching it as a scientific problem to be solved rather than a personal tragedy, he gained a measure of control in an otherwise uncontrollable situation. He started to view his own symptoms as valuable data points in his research, meticulously documenting changes and correlating them with his interactions with the infected.

As the days turned into weeks and months, Sam's determination never wavered. He knew that somewhere in the data, hidden in the complex interplay of neurotransmitters and brain chemistry, lay the key to humanity's survival. And he was determined to find it, no matter how long it took.

Sam faced a daunting challenge in his research: the fundamental mystery at the heart of Parkinson's disease. Despite being first described by James Parkinson in 1817, more than two centuries later, the exact cause of the disorder remained unknown.

This knowledge gap posed a significant barrier to Sam's efforts. How could he unravel the connection between Parkinson's and zombie immunity when the root cause of the disease itself was still unknown? It was like trying to solve a complex equation without knowing one of its key variables.

However, Sam found some encouragement in the progress made in Parkinson's management over the years. Researchers had gained significant ground in understanding the mechanisms of the disease and developing treatments to alleviate its symptoms. This gave him hope that even without knowing the exact cause, meaningful discoveries could still be made.

Sam's analytical mind approached this challenge methodically. He reasoned that if he could identify the specific aspects of Parkinson's that granted immunity, it might shed light on the disease's underlying causes. He began cross-referencing the latest Parkinson's research with his data on zombie interactions, looking for correlations.

He focused on questions like:

Which neurotransmitter changes in Parkinson's patients might be responsible for repelling zombies?

Could the protein aggregates characteristic of Parkinson's be playing a role in the immunity?

How did the progression of Parkinson's symptoms correlate with the strength of the repellent effect?

Despite the frustration of working with incomplete information, Sam remained determined. He knew that his work could provide crucial insights into both the disease and the zombie phenomenon—even if it didn't entirely solve the mystery of Parkinson's. With each piece of data Sam analyzed and each theory he tested, he moved one step closer to unraveling the complex web of Parkinson's disease and its unexpected potential for saving humanity.

***

On May 1, 2032, when Sam met Alex online, their shared desperation for answers bonded them instantly.

Sam leaned in on the video call, his eyes alight with the excitement of sharing his latest hypothesis. "Alex, I think I'm onto something here," he began, his voice low but intense. "We know that people with Parkinson's have significantly lower levels of dopamine in their brains, right?"

Alex nodded, following closely.

"Well," Sam continued, "I've been analyzing the data on zombie behavior and comparing it to what we know about Parkinson's. Here's what I think is happening: The virus that creates the infected seems to target the dopamine pathways in the brain. This causes the aggressive, animalistic behavior we see in the zombies."

Sam paused, making sure Alex was still with him. "Now, here's where it gets interesting. In Parkinson's patients, those dopamine pathways are already compromised. I believe that whatever is causing Parkinson's—and we still don't know exactly what that is—is essentially masking the scents and cues that the infected hunt for in human prey."

"We probably taste funny!" Alex joked. "Parkinson's: Repelling zombies since 1872!"

"No Dad jokes," Sam mumbled, shaking his head.

"Shortly after the initial zombie outbreaks began, I started experiencing bizarre encounters when responding to infected calls," Alex said. "Zombies that came directly face-to-face with me would suddenly stop short right before attacking.

"The first time, I braced myself as an infected staggered toward me, making bloody snarls and clearly hungry for living flesh," Alex continued. "But as it approached me at arm's length, the zombie recoiled, writhing like it had hit an invisible barrier. I provoked a repelled reaction, like identical poles of a magnet.

"I was shocked as the zombie pivoted away, leaving me unscathed. I wrote it off as inexplicable luck. But then it happened again. And again. Whenever the infected got close enough to bite, they would freeze, appearing confused and hurt. Some would grasp their heads, moaning, while others fled from me. It was as if something was warding them off each time at the last moment."

As Alex described the incidents to Sam, the pair speculated on scientific explanations.

"I think it has to do with scents or pheromones repelling the infected," Sam said. "Something in our neurological biology masks us from zombies' detection."

"We need proof," Alex said. "Can we stage some controlled tests?"

"Most certainly!" Sam said with a smile.

Chapter 9: A Meeting of the Minds

Sam's scientific curiosity was piqued by his own experiences and vast amount of research. Meanwhile, Parkinson's disease had somehow granted Alex's apparent zombie immunity. As an analytical thinker, Sam became fixated on isolating the neurological or biological mechanism behind this phenomenon.

He threw himself into the research, forgoing eating and sleeping—and he would have forgone relationships if he had any. As a single man approaching middle age in the middle of a global pandemic, Sam had plenty of time to devote to his new passion.

Beyond intriguing research questions, Sam was struck by the immense implications of this immunity.

"Could this immunity be reproduced for the non-infected?" Sam asked Alex one afternoon on a video call. "This could save millions of people—by a quirk of this devastating disease."

Sam ran computer models analyzing known differences between Parkinson's brains and healthy brains. He pored over the latest Parkinson's research, seeking clues about proteins or enzymes unique to the disease that could alter cells throughout the body.

Late at night, Sam would lose himself in data, feeling so close to revelations that could change everything. While frequently frustrated, he let the guiding purpose behind this research anchor him—to turn neurological adversity into an evolutionary advantage that might just redeem humanity's future.

Sam's priority was pinpointing what specific facet of Parkinson's physiology was interacting with the virus to cloak patients from detection. Was it a certain peptide-blocking receptor? Was it an antibody-triggering inflammatory response? The possibilities fascinated Sam.

Sam knew that the answers could enable scientists to synthesize a protective compound, vaccine, or nanoparticle that mimicked the effects of Parkinson's-altered neurology. This discovery could bring hope to the masses right as it seemed humanity could be facing extinction.

But a moral weight accompanied such power.

"How can we ethically wield this knowledge for good, not exploitation?" Sam asked Alex over Zoom late one night. "I vowed only to pursue science that uplifted humanity as a whole."

Alex agreed. "I'm grappling with all of this morality myself," he confessed.

"What do you mean?" Sam asked.

"Well, it was my own diagnosis that granted me safety in the zombie apocalypse. I've been struggling with serious survivor's guilt because so many of my team members weren't so lucky."

"I can hardly imagine how that must feel," Sam said with a sympathetic nod.

"But if my condition could now shield others, I'm determined to understand and harness this gift," Alex said, mustering a brave smile.

Sam and Alex's shared compassion mattered as much as their intellectual curiosity.

While this discovery gave them hope, many questions still remained. How could they replicate the protective effects for the masses? Were aspects of Parkinson's also the key to a cure? Their work became a race against time as society unraveled.

Chapter 10: United by Disease

After that enlightening video conversation, Alex became obsessed with researching the phenomenon after his own close brushes with the infected. He yearned to connect with others like him who were inexplicably immune.

Alex dove deep into obscure online forums, looking for key terms and snippets that indicated shared experience. Most leads turned up dead ends or unrelatable cases. But he persisted. Late one night, a post caught his eye by a nurse named Mia, who specialized in geriatric patients.

"Anyone else out there with Parkinson's who exhibited infected immunity?"

Alex clicked a link to read Mia's social media profile, where he learned that she worked at a nursing home for people with Parkinson's. Eagerly, he scanned back through all of Mia's posts, which detailed her own improbable zombie immunity. His heart pounded with shock and validation. Her experiences perfectly mirrored his own bizarre close calls.

Alex had feared he was losing his mind making these connections. Yet now here was Mia—someone else putting the same inexplicable, almost supernatural occurrences into words. Alex's hands trembled with adrenaline as he typed a detailed message to her, describing his immunity incidents over the past four years.

Within minutes, a notification popped up—a private message from Mia. Alex could barely contain his excitement clicking on it.

"Hi! Thanks for reaching out! Sounds like we have a lot in common!" Mia wrote.

"Yes," Alex replied. "I thought I was the only one." He felt shell-shocked, out of his body at meeting someone who shared his experiences. Once Alex's initial shock wore off, he began rapidly comparing the specifics of his immunity experience with Mia. The messages flowed quickly, with both of them feeling they could finally speak freely.

"I was so confused the first time a zombie recoiled from me," Mia recounted. "I hadn't yet had any inkling of having Parkinson's. I had run home frantic, looking for some explanation why the infected had ignored me.

"When it happened again, I considered going to a doctor, but I figured they'd dismiss me as delusional," she continued. "So I tested it again. When a third zombie ignored me, I was convinced it was not a coincidence. For some reason, I'm invisible to zombies. It feels surreal. Like I have a superpower."

"I get it," Alex wrote. "I haven't told anyone either because I figured people would think I was crazy, dangerous, or both. Whenever a zombie couldn't sense me, I became more convinced I was going nuts."

"I didn't even tell my parents," Mia typed. "Who would believe that I was somehow invisible to zombies? I already feel conspicuous enough with my trembling and shaking. I didn't want to invite more scrutiny. Plus, I didn't think anyone would believe me. That was soul-crushing." Mia paused, then continued, "I'm sorry. I hope I'm not overwhelming you with my thoughts and emotions. I've been super lonely. Messaging you is helping."

"Not at all," Alex replied. "I understand completely. I appreciate finally having an understanding ear. You run a Parkinson's group? When were you diagnosed?"

"42," Mia wrote, adding a tear emoji.

"I was 40," Alex typed. "It's a gut punch for sure."

"Yes," Mia agreed.

For both Alex and Mia, it was as if the floodgates had burst. They couldn't type their words fast enough.

Tears streamed down Alex's face as he read Mia's vivid accounts, which aligned perfectly with his own. All his endless nights of researching and documenting the phenomenon alone now felt vindicated.

Alex sighed with relief. At last, someone understood the surreal truth that Parkinson's disease seemed to render him invisible to the infected. After years of carrying this burden alone, the euphoric relief of shared understanding was overwhelming. The impossible had become real.

A deep bond formed instantly. Alex knew what it felt like to experience something improbable yet undeniably real. His diagnosis had opened his eyes to hidden dimensions beyond the known world.

Two kindred souls, united by an extraordinary twist of fate, found solace in no longer facing their problems alone. Their friendship soon blossomed into a profound connection, and the future suddenly seemed brighter.

Alex and Mia stayed up all night trading questions and theories and sharing fears and insecurities. With each message, both grew more animated by this first brush with someone who just *got it*. Everything they had bottled up came pouring out.

Mia messaged, "I just finished reviewing one of my patient's files—Mrs. Johnson's. Here's her progression over the last six months." Mia attached an image of the file.

"That bad?" Alex asked as he clicked the file open.

"She was an artist, but now she can barely hold a pen."

"I've been thinking about that a lot lately. How quickly things can change."

"Me too. It's hard not to see our future in these files," Mia agreed. "My aunt started just like us. Early onset. By 50, she couldn't feed herself."

"I keep thinking about my grandmother. Watching her decline. I didn't really understand what she was going through back then," Alex said. "Now I do."

"Now we understand too well," Mia agreed. "I have a recurring nightmare—I'm putting in an IV, and my hands won't stop shaking."

"Mine is being on a call. Someone's coding, and I can't move fast enough to help," Alex said, nodding in understanding. "Really messes with your head, doesn't it?"

"Every day," Mia typed. "At least we're not alone in this."

"True. Makes it a little easier, knowing someone else gets it."

"Think we'll find anything in all this research? Something that could help?"

"Have to believe we will. Otherwise, what's the point?"

"Yeah," Mia typed wistfully. "You should get some sleep. You have an early day tomorrow."

"You too. Don't stay up all night reading files."

"Look who's talking! Goodnight, Alex."

"Night, Mia. Try to get some rest."

***

Within a day, Alex and Mia's dialogue shifted from medical curiosity to a profound personal connection. Their shared revelation erased years of suppressed isolation. Two kindred souls had found each other through the improbable quirks of a disease.

Alex's empty search had unexpectedly landed precisely who he needed—someone whose experiences mirrored his own. With this discovery came a sense of belonging that he had lost long ago. Two strangers had found a home in the most unlikely place.

***

A few nights later, the pair's conversation continued, this time over video chat. For the first time Alex saw Mia—a 5-foot 2-inch redhead with pale skin, brilliant blue eyes, and a natural beauty that left no need for makeup. Like most people, Alex thought Mia to be an extrovert due to her friendly nature, which belied her true introversion.

As Alex was silently admiring Mia's good looks, she began to speak. "My sister, Sarah Thomas, is a neurochemist studying Parkinson's at the University of Michigan. Her research indicates it's the dopamine deficiency in Parkinson's patients that might render zombies unable to detect them. The missing neurotransmitter acts as a cloaking mechanism."

Mia explained to Alex that Sarah ran a prestigious neurology research lab at the university's medical center. As a tenured professor and leading researcher in neurodegenerative diseases, she had significant autonomy in choosing her research assistants.

The pair hatched a plan that perhaps they take some time off and go to Michigan to help Sarah with her research.

"Let me ask her if we could help," Mia said. "I'll get back to you, Alex."

***

When Mia approached Sarah about the pair traveling to help in the lab, Sarah recognized the unique value of having a nurse and an EMT, both with firsthand Parkinson's experience, assisting with her research.

"It's certainly unconventional, but I don't see why I can't get this request approved," Sarah told Mia.

Sarah's lab was a state-of-the-art facility on the third floor of the University of Michigan's medical research building. It was filled with advanced imaging equipment, processing stations, and a dedicated space for tissue sample analysis. Sarah's grant funding ensured the lab had access to cutting-edge technology and resources needed for their research.

Sara used her authority as lab director to secure official research assistant positions for both Mia and Alex. Their medical backgrounds allowed her to fast-track the necessary clearances and training requirements. Although it was unusual to bring in outside medical professionals as lab assistants, Sarah convinced the department that their practical experience with Parkinson's patients—and of course their own diagnoses—made them invaluable to her research.

***

Both Alex and Mia were able to burn some long-saved vacation time to make the trip to the university. The close friends met for the first time in the airport, then caught an Uber together to ride to Sarah's lab.

Upon meeting Sarah for the first time, Alex was struck by her similarities to Mia. Sarah was a slightly blonder, taller, and older version of his already dear friend.

Alex was eager to learn more about Mia and also to get to know her sister. That first night, they talked late into the evening. The conversation started with work, then meandered to their childhoods.

"I grew up in Brooklyn, New York," Alex said. "My high school graduating class was a sea of thousands.

"We're from the Midwest," Mia and Sarah said at the same time.

"Our whole hometown had just 700 residents," Mia said.

"There were only twenty-five students in my graduating class," Sarah added.

Alex was stunned and flooded with questions, baffled by the idea of such a small community.

"Everyone knew each other's business," Sarah joked. "The diner ran out of pie every day at 1 p.m. sharp."

Alex wondered, *How could such a world exist so differently from everything I know?*

Mia and Sarah regaled Alex with tales of quaint traditions and customs that underscored the charm and character of small-town ways—market days when everyone gathered on the square to trade handicrafts and catch up on gossip and seasonal festivals that celebrated local harvests and history.

One tale that caught Alex completely off guard was the crowning of a Corn King at county fairs. Whichever boy husked an ear with the biggest kernel earned this honor and bragging rights for the year. Alex shook his head in amused disbelief.

The tales of grassroots life evoked nostalgia in Mia and Sarah, but they left city boy Alex feeling like he'd entered a foreign land. He had many questions about their Huck Finn–like childhoods. But mostly, he marveled at the magic of their little quaint community trappings that enriched their lives in ways Alex struggled to grasp.

That night, Alex enjoyed his glimpse into Mia and Sarah's beginnings that were so vastly different from his own concrete jungle origins. Their shared laughter as colleagues fused once-distant worlds into their story unfolding together.

Alex could feel the tiredness overtaking him. "I think you broke me with all this country talk," he yawned and laughed at the same time.

Mia and Sarah smiled knowingly at each other. Alex was clearly a fish out of water regarding their agricultural roots. But they enjoyed opening his eyes to a world beyond the big city.

Their camaraderie provided a rare light moment amidst the chaos still spiraling out of control across the country. For a brief time, the friends could chat about old memories rather than the crisis at hand. No matter their differences, they were bonded in this fight together.

After their spirited stroll down memory lane, Alex, Mia, and Sarah went to get a good night's sleep, knowing their lab tasks would begin early the next day. Sarah retired to her nearby apartment, and she showed Alex and Mia to a suite she had commandeered for them in a newly built but as yet unused university dorm.

The next day, as the trio sat hunched over microscopes analyzing samples, each mind buzzed with new tidbits learned about the others' pasts. At times in the weeks ahead, they would become so engrossed with the technical minutiae of their research that they would forget the people behind the pipettes. But that day, vivid glimpses of Mia and Sarah's small-town roots made them feel more whole to Alex—not just colleagues but new friends.

There was still so much left to discover about the winding paths that merged their lives here. How many more treasured memories and formative moments remained unseen beneath the surface? Uncovering those layers felt every bit as precious as the science itself.

As much as their research aimed to protect humanity on a global scale, these quiet glimpses into their shared humanity truly nourished their spirits. Like the lingering aroma of a home-cooked meal, those moments left them feeling connected, seen, and cared for.

The kernel of deeper understanding they planted together would germinate slowly over time into a sturdy oak of friendship under whose branches they could always find refuge. There would be room for both hard science and nostalgic musings of youth within these walls.

As the trio worked, residual glimpses of Mia and Sarah's humble beginnings lingered like motes swirling through sunbeams. Details of the friends, hideouts, customs, and capers that colored their innocent years continued percolating even amidst microscope adjustments and reagent preparation.

After years laser-focused on driving cutting-edge research, this rearview look into their unassuming rural roots sparked renewed appreciation for the unlikely stargazers and adventurers who paved this future path.

As enrapt children watching cloud shapes transform, who could have predicted the three pioneering the scientific frontier to defend humanity? They had simply followed each spark of wonder or inspiration that lit through the years.

Yet tracing the thread back revealed how profoundly those small-town days shaped the intrepid hearts now tasked with wrestling life from calamity's maw. The seeds of perseverance through long odds, compassion for neighbors as family, and awe of nature's mysteries already dwell within youthful dreamers gazing heavenward for their one allotted wish.

However starry-eyed their childhood dreams under boundless skies, reality had birthed this unimaginable fate as guardians of all they held dear. And the humble origins they now rediscovered deepened their commitment to carrying others over hope's horizon through this endless night.

When Alex glanced sidelong to catch Mia and Sarah mid-laugh, he glimpsed once more the guileless spirits who first awakened their noble crusade. And he knew then that sometimes heroes arise not in spite of wide-eyed innocence, but because of it.

Chapter 11: Chemistry Labs

As Alex and Mia spent more time together working in the lab, a natural chemistry developed between them. The lab became their sanctuary, a place where they could pursue answers while finding comfort in each other's company. They often worked late into the night, their conversations shifting from medical observations to more personal matters as they huddled in a small tea nook Sarah had set up in the corner of the lab.

That cozy spot, with its electric kettle and collection of mismatched mugs, became Alex and Mia's favorite retreat. There, surrounded by the gentle hum of equipment and the faint scent of Earl Grey, they found themselves opening up about their fears, hopes, and experiences with Parkinson's. Within the sterile, scientific environment of the lab, the little nook provided an oddly intimate setting for their growing connection.

Sarah observed their budding relationship with quiet approval, recognizing that their personal investment in the research and deepening bond could only benefit their work. She gave them increasing autonomy in the lab, trusting their dedication to the research, appreciating how their unique perspectives enhanced her team's understanding of Parkinson's disease, and happy for her sister to have found such a special pair-bond.

One late night in the lab, equipment hummed softly in the background as Mia and Alex sat in the tea nook. Each cradled steaming mugs of tea.

"You know what I admire about you?" Mia asked suddenly, breaking the comfortable silence. Alex looked up, surprised by the question.

Without waiting for an answer, Mia continued, "The way you approach your patients. Even with everything you're dealing with yourself, you're still so focused on helping others."

Alex's warm brown eyes met Mia's bright blue ones. "I could say the same about you. Most people who've watched Parkinson's devastate their family would run as far and fast from it as possible. But here you are, diving deeper into understanding it."

"Sometimes I wonder if I'm trying to make up for feeling so helpless watching my aunt, my grandmother ... knowing there was nothing I could do to stop it," Mia admitted, her fingers tracing the rim of her mug.

"Is that why you became a nurse?"

"Partly. I thought if I could understand it better, maybe ..." Mia's voice trailed off. Then she shook her head. "But now here I am, facing the same darned thing."

"But you're not running from it," Alex said softly. "That takes courage."

"Neither are you," Mia pointed out. "Most guys I know would be drowning in self-pity by now. But you're still working in this lab every single day, and every single night you're scouring the internet, looking for answers."

"I guess we're both a little crazy that way," Alex said, smiling.

"Maybe," Mia said, returning Alex's smile and tucking a strand of red hair behind one ear. "It's nice to meet someone who gets it. Finally. Who understands why this matters so much."

"The research?"

"All of it. The patients, the mysteries, the need to make some kind of difference while we still can." Mia paused, meeting Alex's eyes. "Most people don't understand that drive."

"No," Alex agreed quietly. "They don't."

The pair sat in companionable silence for a moment, both understanding that something deeper than professional collaboration was growing between them.

"We should probably get back to those samples," Mia said finally, though she made no move to leave.

"Probably," Alex agreed, nodding, equally reluctant to break the spell. "I'm glad you're here. That we're doing this together."

"Me too, Alex. Me too."

In Alex, Mia found refuge sharing youthful dreams once scorned about daring discoveries to revolutionize awful diseases. And Alex discovered grace again through Mia's resilience tempered by past trials. As humanity faced catastrophe around them, furtive hopes bloomed anew from ashes where both had long forsworn possibilities of intimacy again.

Laughter came easier behind their sealed lab doors insulating them in a private world of light still being kindled against the spreading darkness. Each night walking back to the dorm, Mia lingered longer with Alex, gazing skyward before their fingers intertwined at last. Cautious optimism stirred that out of even this nightmare springing from the quirks of Parkinson's, providence had gifted them each other.

United by devotion in various forms, selfless and profound, Alex and Mia fought alongside Sarah for scientific breakthroughs that could forestall mankind's end. But in precious hidden moments, longing looks illuminated deeper yearnings finally being requited. Come tragedy or triumph, this gift of unexpected love consecrated all sacrifices ahead, binding their linked futures into destiny's tale still unfolding.

Chapter 12: State of the Crisis

Five years into the pandemic, society had restructured itself around the zombie threat. Major cities like New York and Los Angeles had been divided into distinct zones—the heavily fortified "safe zones" where most of the population lived and worked, and the "wild zones" where the infected roamed unchecked through empty streets and abandoned buildings.

The safe zones operated like military installations, with thirty-foot reinforced walls topped with razor wire and illuminated by motion-activated UV lights. Armed military police at checkpoints controlled all movements in and out and conducted strict decontamination protocols and biometric screening for anyone seeking entry. Armed patrols monitored the walls 24/7, while surveillance drones tracked infected movements in the surrounding areas.

Despite these precautions, the casualty numbers remained sobering. Global statistics reported fifty to seventy-five confirmed zombie attacks each day. However, experts believed the figure could be two or three times higher when accounting for unreported incidents in rural areas and developing nations. Even New York, with its state-of-the-art containment systems, averaged three or four incidents daily—usually from the infected breaching weak points in the perimeter and hiding in supposedly cleared buildings.

Most of the zombie attacks occurred in the gray zones between the safe and wild areas—the partially secured neighborhoods where people still lived, but with limited protection. These areas served as buffer zones, and they had become the refuge for people who couldn't afford the steep cost of living in the safe zones or for those who refused to abandon their homes.

The daily reports of missing persons and zombie sightings had become as routine as weather forecasts. They were a grim reminder that humanity's foothold against the zombies remained precarious—even after five years of adaptation and fortification.

Across the globe, government responses to the zombie crisis varied dramatically. Even each state in the United States had significant autonomy in managing its own safe zones, although federal guidelines established minimum security protocols. Europe adopted a more unified approach, with the EU coordinating containment efforts across borders. Asia saw the strictest measures, with China and Japan converting entire cities into fortress-like compounds.

As the years passed, movement restrictions became increasingly sophisticated. Citizens were assigned security clearance levels that detailed which areas within the safe zones they could access. Digital tracking systems monitored population movement, while mandatory health screenings checked for signs of infection. Travel between cities required extensive paperwork, medical clearance, and often quarantine periods of up to two weeks.

The scientific community's efforts to understand and combat the zombie threat remained fragmented. In the United States, major research institutions focused on different aspects of the crisis. The Centers for Disease Control and Prevention studied zombie physiology and transmission methods, while universities investigated the zombies' behavioral patterns and potential environment factors. Private pharmaceutical companies raced to develop vaccines, and military researchers explored weapons and containment strategies.

Despite the billions of dollars that were being spent, progress was glacially slow and terribly limited. Early vaccine attempts either failed to prevent zombification or caused severe neurological side effects. Treatments showed some promise in slowing the infection's progress but couldn't reverse it. The most effective breakthrough came in the form of enhanced detection methods, allowing security forces to identify infected individuals before they turned.

Meanwhile, pharmaceutical companies faced mounting pressure to produce results, leading to several rushed trials that ended in disaster. These failures further eroded public trust in official response efforts and fueled growing underground markets for unproven treatments and protection methods.

Even inside the safe zones, people lived under constant threat. The adaptations were severe, and necessary markets operated only during daylight hours, schools ran on hybrid schedules, and most nonessential work remained remote. Underground networks flourished, with speakeasies, black markets, and unofficial information channels helping people cope with the restrictions.

Despite containment efforts, the infected seemed to be growing more numerous. Zombie sightings increased steadily—even in previously secured areas. This led to expanded military presence in many cities and stricter enforcement of safety protocols.

Meanwhile, more and more people noticed that zombies displayed unusual behavior around certain people, particularly those with neurological conditions. Authorities largely dismissed these incidents as coincidental, but underground forums buzzed with theories and speculation.

Of course, this wasn't a surprise to Alex, Mia, and Sarah—and Sam, whom Alex had recently looped into their work. Still, they kept their research into and discoveries about Parkinson's patients' immunity closely guarded. They feared that premature exposure would lead to either exploitation of vulnerable patients or interference with their research. The small team agreed that until they better understood the mechanism behind the immunity and could protect it from misuse, silence was their safest option.

Alex and his team closely monitored the public's discussions about a possible link between neurological conditions and zombie immunity. Even though they had decided not to go public—for now—they watched for patterns that might support their research. Still they were careful not to draw attention to their own findings.

As another year of the crisis unfolded, humanity clung to whatever normalcy it could find while adapting to an increasingly dangerous world. In their trying-to-fly-under-the-radar lab, Alex and his team raced against time, hoping to unlock the secrets of their immunity before the growing zombie threat overwhelmed humanity's defenses.

Chapter 13: Shaky Squad

Several years had passed since Alex and Sam had connected over their shared Parkinson's diagnoses. Alex had invited Sam many times to join them in Michigan, to no avail. Sam was comfortable and content where he was and had no desire to travel. As often as Alex could, he pulled Sam into conversations with Mia and Sarah and kept him up to speed on their lab research. Despite being separated by distance, Sam had proven to be an invaluable member of the team.

Despite their frequent contact, Alex worried about his friend's isolation. One evening over Zoom, he broached the topic. "I've been thinking. There must be others out there like us. People with Parkinson's who've noticed this immunity thing."

"They're probably scared and confused, just like we were, with no one to talk to about it," Sam nodded.

"Exactly. What if we created some kind of online support group? Something secure where people could share their experiences."

"Could be risky. If the wrong people found out ... but I could set up encrypted channels, careful screening protocols. Make it look like just another Parkinson's support network on the surface," Sam said, starting to sound a little bit excited.

"But underneath, it would be a way for people like us to connect."

"Yeah. Think about it—I'm seeing more and more posts online about people who've noticed this pattern. And these people need support, especially the newly diagnosed," Sam said.

"It would help us gather more data too. More cases to study."

"Right. Plus, there's strength in numbers."

"Let's do it. But we'll need to be careful about who we let in," Alex said.

"Already working on a verification system. We'll start small, build trust gradually."

"This could make a real difference for people who think they're going crazy, seeing zombies ignore them."

"Exactly. Give them hope, understanding, and maybe some answers."

"When can we start?" Alex asked, smiling at how well this conversation was going.

"Give me a few days to set up the secure infrastructure. Then we can begin reaching out."

"Alright. Let's give these people somewhere to turn. God knows we could've used that in the beginning."

Neither Alex or Sam had experience building online communities, so it was clumsy trial and error. Despite Sam's technical savvy, it took them weeks to figure out how to work the video call settings. By the time they figured things out, a motley crew of members had found their way in.

Henry Thompson, sixty-eight, had been a beloved literature professor at the University of Virginia for more than three decades. His first symptoms appeared during lectures—a slight tremor in his hand while writing on the blackboard. Students began noticing his increasingly shuffling gait between classes. A proud academic, he initially attributed these changes to age, until a colleague gently suggested he seek medical attention. His early retirement was prompted not by the physical symptoms, but by the cognitive fog that made it difficult to recall his beloved literary quotes. Now he found solace in sharing his experiences with others, often relating their struggles to themes in classic literature.

Grace Chen, forty-two, had been a rising star in Los Angeles theater and a sought-after yoga instructor. Her diagnosis came after students noticed her unusual stiffness during demonstrations and her increasingly frequent balance issues during poses. The tremors eventually made it impossible to maintain the precise movements required for both acting and yoga. Rather than leave the spotlight entirely, Grace channeled her creative energy into advocacy, using her performance background to create compelling social media content about living with young-onset Parkinson's. Her sessions often included tips for adapting yoga poses for others with PD.

Dot Anderson, seventy-three, had run her famous fudge shop in Minneapolis for more than forty years. Her handmade treats were legendary, with secret recipes passed down through generations. When the tremors began, she tried to adapt, using different tools and working during her "on" periods when medications were most effective. But after several batches of candy were ruined by her shaking hands, she made the heartbreaking decision to close the shop. The recipes remained unshared because she could no longer demonstrate the precise techniques required. Her contributions to the group often centered around finding new ways to preserve one's legacy when traditional paths are no longer possible.

Lisa Martinez, thirty-five, was a former elementary school teacher who had to step away from the classroom after her diagnosis at thirty-two. As a stay-at-home mom to three young children, she struggled with both managing her symptoms and explaining her condition to her kids. Her youngest was born just months after her diagnosis, making the early years of motherhood especially challenging. She brought practical insights to the group about parenting with PD, like how to handle playground visits during "off" periods or explain tremors to curious children. Her natural optimism and problem-solving attitude helped newer members see that life could still be rich and meaningful, even if differently than planned.

The early video chats were painfully quiet—with just that handful of people staring at each other, searching for conversation starters about life with PD.

After an awkward silence in one video chat, Grace shifted uncomfortably, her neck muscles visibly contracting. "You know what's interesting? How differently this thing hits each of us. I see some of your hands shaking, but that's not really my battle."

Henry looked down at his trembling right hand and said, "Yeah, the tremors are my constant companion. Can't seem to shake them. No pun intended."

"Meanwhile, I'm dealing with these damned muscle contractions," Grace said. "My neck and shoulder just ... seize up. Dystonia's a real pain."

"That's what's wild about Parkinson's—same disease, completely different symptoms. My movements are all over the place with the tremors, but you're dealing with muscle rigidity," Dot added.

"Tell me about it. Some days I can barely turn my head," Grace said. "But it looks like for you it's the opposite—like your body won't stop moving even when you want it to."

Alex, who was facilitating the group that evening, joined in, "Tremor dominant versus dystonia dominant. That's what the doctors call it, right?"

"Yeah. Makes it hard to explain to people sometimes," Grace said. "They see you shake and think, 'That's Parkinson's.' But for me, unless they catch me when my neck is spasming ..."

"They might not think anything's wrong at all," Alex finished her sentence.

"Exactly." Grace paused as her neck muscles contracted again. "Though right now it's pretty obvious."

"Hey, at least between the two of us, we've got the full Parkinson's experience covered," Henry said, holding up his shaking hand.

"Maybe that's why we make a good team. You shake, I seize, but together we keep pushing forward," Grace quipped.

The rest of the group nodded and smiled in agreement.

Later that evening after the support group Zoom had ended, Alex Zoomed with Sam. "Let's keep getting this support group off the ground."

"Yeah. Though maybe we should warn people they're getting advice from one guy who can't turn his head and another who can't hold his coffee steady."

"Hey, who better to understand what they're going through?"

The friends shared knowing looks, their initial awkwardness long forgotten in the understanding that despite their different symptoms, they were both fighting the same battle.

Over the next few months, Alex and Sam persisted in growing their fledgling group, posting in PD forums and social media groups to spread the word about their new support group. They customized flyers to hang with tremoring hands in neurologist offices and pharmacies.

Slowly, their efforts paid off, and each week, a few new faces joined the video calls. The technology still proved to be a steep learning curve, but the desire for connection overcame the technical difficulties.

Soon, Alex and Sam established a format for the support group Zooms, beginning with introductions and personal updates, then sharing resources and tips as the discussion flowed. The more diverse voices joined in, the more animated the conversations grew.

Alex and Sam were moved to see bonds blossom between people brought together by circumstance. Their shared purpose eclipsed early growing pains. Each week, the group felt more like a family coming home, and the voices grew louder with laughter, empathy, and encouragement.

"I think we've created something special here," Alex said one evening on the call after everyone but Sam had dropped off.

"What a deep well of resilience," Sam agreed.

"Even small actions to lift others up can spark ripples of hope, touching more lives than we know."

Each new member to the PD support group brought unique perspectives and experiences, creating a tapestry of support that went far beyond their shared diagnosis. Their stories illustrated how Parkinson's affects people across all walks of life, while their collective wisdom helped each person navigate their own journeys with the disease.

It was an eclectic mix of people, but illness doesn't discriminate. Each week, new members joined, drawn in by the community's welcoming spirit. Their stories inspired Alex, reminding him that if people support each other, life can flourish even amidst loss.

As the video support group's attendance grew, subgroups formed around shared interests, such as exercise, nutrition, and advocacy. Friendships blossomed between members. The eye-rolling jokes and candid vulnerability revealed shared understanding and compassion.

Many support group members appreciated using the others as a sounding board for their symptoms and condition. Even before the pandemic, PD patients saw their neurologists only twice a year because there were only 743 movement disorder specialists to diagnose and treat the more than one million diagnosed in the United States. During the pandemic, those doctor visits became even more difficult to make because people had to weigh the rewards of seeing their MDs against the risks of leaving the relative safety of their homes.

Providing those benefits to the group made Alex proud, as he watched participants motivate each other through obstacles big and small. He remembered how alone he had felt at his own diagnosis. Creating this group to lift up others gave him a sense of purpose amidst the uncertainty Parkinson's brought.

As months passed, Alex and Sam's support group expanded through word of mouth and creative outreach efforts. Before long, they had regular members joining the group from countries around the globe.

Spanning time zones became tricky, but Sam devised a schedule to cycle meeting times so everyone could participate live at some point. Translating materials was a hurdle too, but they made it work with automated services and a fantastic volunteer translator team.

The diversity was awe-inspiring for Alex and Sam. They were humbled by the realization that countless people worldwide were navigating life with Parkinson's too. Theirs was no longer an isolated battle—but a far-reaching human experience.

Of course, challenges and opinions varied across cultures and backgrounds. Not everyone had access to the same resources or community acceptance. But the heart of the group remained unchanged—people coming together in search of connection, hope, and understanding.

During every meeting, Alex felt how Parkinson's simultaneously created division from the world, yet also bound this global community together. While part of their identity was defined by illness, it was not the whole of who they were. Their shared humanity mattered infinitely more.

Seeing members lift each other up with empathy, humor, and encouragement was the true reward. More than any one individual, this collective resilience spoke to the power of courageous spirits coming together.

In darker moments of doubt, Alex would reflect on the network's unwavering heart. It centered him again, knowing he was part of something greater—a human mosaic that revealed beauty not despite its fragmented pieces, but because of them.

Little did Alex know how important these kindred spirits would become on his journey ahead. When the darkness fell, Alex's motley crew would ignite the flame in his much-needed lighthouse.

Chapter 14: Labors of Progress

As the world seemed to get more chaotic by the minute, in the quiet of Sarah's lab, the trio tirelessly continued their research. After years of work, Sarah's breakthrough research about Parkinson's biomarkers—measurable indicators of the disease—sparked a flurry of activity. Finally, the team had a promising trail to follow.

Now more than ever, Mia's nursing experience in neurology became invaluable. Together, the sisters worked to identify the most potent immuno-cloaking compounds that were produced by Parkinson's neurobiology.

"I'm starting to think that certain proteins or enzymes must hold the key to camouflaging cells from the infected," Sarah said.

"That's huge," Mia said. "But now we have to figure out which one!"

The team wanted to continue to keep their research secret, but they had been carefully vetting and screening all new members to their online support group. Slowly and carefully, Alex began to share information about their research with especially trusted members of the support group. Members discreetly shared information with other Parkinson's patients they trusted, and slowly a pool formed of willing participants who understood the importance of their work.

Together with Sarah, Alex and Mia began collecting comprehensive biological samples from volunteers they identified via an underground network. Volunteers traveled to Sarah's lab in Ann Arbor, Michigan, or Henry's lab in Charlottesville, Virginia, for intensive tests, including skin biopsies to analyze cellular changes, spinal taps to study cerebrospinal fluid composition, and DaTscans to measure dopamine transporter levels. Blood samples were also collected to examine various biomarkers and protein levels.

When each sample was received at their Michigan lab, Mia meticulously cataloged it, creating detailed profiles for every participant. Her records included the biological data and also comprehensive patient histories: time since diagnosis, progression of symptoms, medication responses, and notably, any experiences with zombie encounters. These detailed histories helped the team track patterns between neurological changes and immunity effects.

The support group proved invaluable in the effort to find study participants. Henry used his academic connections. Grace leveraged her social media presence, and Dot mined her business networks to find more participants. Each new volunteer brought the team closer to understanding the mysterious link between Parkinson's and zombie immunity.

As more and more samples arrived from across the country, Sarah's lab became a hub of activity. The team worked carefully to maintain the samples' anonymity while processing the invaluable biological materials that might hold the key to humanity's survival.

In a surprisingly short period of time, the growing database of neurological signatures began to reveal intriguing patterns about how Parkinson's altered the body's chemical signals in ways that seemed to repel the infected.

Long days in the lab blurred together, and frustration inevitably arose. Mia kept everyone's spirits high with her passionate curiosity for unraveling Parkinson's disease mysteries that had plagued her family for so long.

During one extended trial that yet again failed to uncover the elusive protein or enzyme responsible for shielding PD patients, Alex was surprised to see Mia smiling calmly as she rearranged lab equipment.

"We're getting closer," Mia said with quiet confidence.

Alex smiled in return, inspired by her unshakable grit. To her, failure was fuel to keep iterating.

Late one night in the lab, Mia looked up at Alex from her microscope with an expression of wonder. "You know what amazes me? How something we think of as a disease—as damage—could actually create these protective compounds."

"What do you mean?" Alex asked, looking up from his notes that were spread all over the table in front of him.

"It's like nature found a way to turn our broken dopamine system into a shield. Even if it wasn't intentional, is it a gift?"

"It's pretty ironic that our biggest challenge somehow became our greatest defense."

"Exactly!" Mia said. "All these complex biological processes we're studying—they're like an intricate dance we never knew existed until now."

"You really love this stuff, don't you? The science behind it all."

"I can't help it. Even with everything we're dealing with—the symptoms, the uncertainty—there's something beautiful about understanding how it all works."

"Even when that understanding comes from studying our own disease?"

"Maybe *especially* then. We're not just solving a puzzle, Alex. We're finding meaning in our suffering. We're using it to help others."

"Sometimes suffering seems like it," Alex said. "I'm glad you can find some meaning in it. I never thought about it that way. I've been so focused on finding a solution."

"The solution will come. It helps me to not wallow in my own problems when I can step back and appreciate the complexity of what we're studying. It helps me remember why we're doing this."

"To reduce suffering wherever we can?" Alex asked, smiling.

"And to understand the marvelous complexities of our world. Even the painful ones."

Alex and Mia shared a moment of comfortable silence, both contemplating how their personal struggles had led them to these profound discoveries—and to this memorable moment.

Together, Alex and Mia poured all their free time over molecular models, tinkered with refractory equipment, and parsed data, looking for clues. Their coffee intake spiked along with reagent expenditures. Meals became takeout haphazardly shared between experiments, accompanied by spirited discussions of confounding test results.

In the windowless lab, Alex soon lost track of day versus night. Time blurred into a cycle of trial and error, intellectual debate, sparks of inspiration, and demoralizing setbacks. But even incremental progress buoyed the team's momentum.

After weeks of fruitless experiments hitting dead end after dead end, frustrations were running high in the lab. Morale was dipping, and the team began to lose faith they would ever pin down the elusive immuno-cloaking compound.

During one late-night research session, Alex noticed Mia intently examining a molecular model of an enzyme found in unusually high concentrations in Parkinson's patients.

Her eyes suddenly lit up with excitement. Turning to Alex with a grin, she exclaimed, "I think this could be it!"

"What?" Alex asked, Mia's enthusiasm instantly reigniting his lagging hopes.

"Let's go tell Sam," Mia said, grabbing Alex by the hand and pulling him out of the lab to the office to video conference Sam.

After Sam was looped in, he ran computer simulations on the enzyme's theoretical interactions. The results predicted the enzyme would bind to certain scent receptors in the zombies, keeping them from smelling the dopamine and detecting the people who don't have Parkinson's!

Now that the team had identified the enzyme, even more work was ahead. For the next many months, the team extracted and refined the enzyme from volunteers. They then developed what they believed was a viable cloaking compound. They carefully altered the enzyme's molecular structure to enhance its binding capabilities and extend its active duration in the bloodstream. Finally, after painstaking effort, they were able to produce sufficient quantity to test it on one non-infected, non-Parkinson's affected person.

Now that the team had something to test, they had a new worry. They *could* test. But *should* they?

For days, the team debated the ethics and risks involved.

After late coffee-fueled discussions, and restless sleepless nights, the team reached a unanimous decision.

Yes, we should test.

But who?

"I'm the logical first test subject," Sarah volunteered. "For goodness' sake, I'm the only one here without Parkinson's."

"Please, no," Mia objected.

"I'm not sure that it makes sense to risk your health," Alex agreed.

"No. As the lead researcher, it's my responsibility to assume the risk," Sarah shut down their objections.

The trial protocol was meticulously planned. Alex converted an abandoned isolation room from the university's hospital into a controlled testing environment—a reinforced glass enclosure with a sealed airlock system and other reinforced safety measures. In the next room, behind multiple security doors, they kept two contained infected subjects—former hospital patients who had turned and been captured by emergency services during a recent outbreak.

On a Tuesday morning, Sarah received the injection. For six hours, Alex and Mia monitored her vitals and took regular blood samples to track the compound's dispersion through her system. When all of Sarah's biomarkers indicated optimal saturation, they proceeded to the exposure phase.

The team fitted Sarah with biosensors and a panic button that would trigger immediate extraction. Multiple cameras had been set up in the isolation room to record the encounter from every angle. Alex and Sam would both monitor Sarah's safety from their computers.

Sarah entered the controlled exposure chamber. Once she was locked inside, Alex remotely opened the connecting door to the infected holding area.

The first infected subject shambled in, its movements erratic but purposeful, scanning the room. Alex quickly closed the door behind the zombie. Sarah stood perfectly still, and on the monitors Alex could see her heart rate elevated but steady. The infected moved closer to Sarah, seemingly drawn to her presence.

Then came the moment they'd all been waiting for. At approximately two meters' distance, the infected suddenly paused. It tilted its head, appearing confused. It circled Sarah at that perimeter, never approaching closer and occasionally making frustrated vocalizations.

When the second infected was introduced, it exhibited the same behavior—initial interest followed by confusion and avoidance. Neither subject attempted to attack Sarah, despite her presence in the very room with them.

After twenty excruciating minutes, Alex and Mia entered the room and stood between Sarah and the zombies to obfuscate the zombie's scent while Sarah was able to safely exit the chamber.

"We did it!" Mia cheered. "The modified enzyme compound replicated the natural cloaking effect of PD in Sarah, who thank goodness doesn't have Parkinson's!"

***

The celebration was short-lived.

Within hours, Sarah began experiencing concerning side effects—severe headaches, tremors, and cognitive confusion. By evening, she exhibited symptoms remarkably similar to acute Parkinson's disease. The compound had successfully mimicked the protective aspect of the disease, and its debilitating effects as well.

Fortunately, Sarah's side effects were only temporary. A few hours later, they began to fade due to the compound's short half-life.

This sobering reality forced the team back to the drawing board. They had proven their theory correct, but the cloaking results needed to be more consistent and longer lasting. Their elusive goal remained to create a solution that protected *without* harming.

During one trial, the compound wore off unexpectedly while the infected still surrounded Sarah.

"Sarah! Move NOW!" Alex shouted into the comms.

"The compound's wearing off," Sarah's voice came through, trembling. "They're starting to notice me."

"I see it," Alex said, more calmly than he felt. "Just keep your eyes on the exit. I'm creating a diversion." Frantically, he began banging on a metal pipe against the far wall to create a distraction for the zombies to buy Sarah some time

Sam's voice cut in. "Alex, what are you doing? Stick to the extraction protocol!"

"No time," Alex replied, continuing to make as much noise as possible. "Sarah, on my count. Three ... two ... one ... GO!"

The security feed showed Sarah making a mad dash for the exit as the infected turned toward Alex's distraction. Sarah slipped through the door just as one of the zombies lunged in her direction.

Once the security doors sealed and the team regrouped in the lab, the adrenaline gave way to horrified realization.

"That was too close," Mia said, handing Sarah a blanket as she shivered from shock.

"The compound degraded completely after only seventeen minutes," Sam noted, reviewing the data on his tablet. "Way faster than our projections."

"I could feel it happening," Sarah said, still fighting to catch her breath. "One minute they couldn't sense me, the next it was like a switch flipped. They just ... focused on me."

Alex paced around the room, running his hands through his hair. "We can't risk this again. Not until we've stabilized the formula."

"But we're so close," Sarah argued. "The initial cloaking effect worked perfectly."

"Right up until it nearly got you killed," Mia countered firmly.

"This isn't just about scientific progress anymore," Alex said, his voice heavy with the weight of what had nearly happened. "We're playing with fire here. Real lives are at stake."

Sam nodded solemnly. "Alex is right. We're getting ahead of ourselves. We need to perfect this before any more human trials. The hazards are just too great."

"Back to the lab then," Sarah conceded, still visibly shaken. "But what we learned today proves we're on the right track."

"Yeah," Alex said, the image of the infected lunging toward Sarah looming large in his mind. "But next time, we make damn sure it works before putting anyone in that room again."

Though progress felt within reach, the setbacks left the team as focused as ever. Their purpose had crystallized—not just experimenting in a lab but urgently seeking to shield humanity from a terrifying threat. Failure was not an option when so much hung in the balance.

Invigorated by hope and greater understanding, their perseverance redoubled. Even incremental steps brought them closer to solutions that could forever change the fate of humankind.

After months of intense effort, the first successful test of their cloaking compound felt like a miraculous breakthrough. As the reality sunk in, Alex turned to see Mia watching the infected trial with tears glistening in her eyes.

In that moment, surrounded by lab equipment and computers, the humanity behind their efforts suddenly took center stage. Wordlessly, Alex embraced Mia as joyful tears streamed down both their faces.

Since this journey began, they had sacrificed so much—personal lives, safety, comfort. The endless hours spent working in secret had strained even their strong spirits.

But here was proof it had not been in vain. Their perseverance and collective knowledge had led them one step closer to saving untold lives. Hope could spread its wings again thanks to what they had built together.

Standing amidst the sterile machines and bottles that had consumed their days, Alex was flooded with gratitude for the heart and soul each person brought to this mission. Their bonds ran deeper than research for its own sake.

In Mia's tear-filled eyes, Alex glimpsed the gravity of what they were pursuing. Amidst death and despair, they had kindled new life.

"We're going to do this," Alex told Mia, pulling her close.

For the first time, the finish line seemed within reach. Doubt still lingered, but the team was buoyed by possibility and a spirit of unity. Whatever lay ahead, Alex knew they would face it as one.

Chapter 15: The Bonds of Love

Alex and Mia's natural chemistry became increasingly evident as they worked closely analyzing lab results. The lab hummed with equipment noise as they moved around each other with the comfortable familiarity of dance partners.

"Hand me that slide, would you?" Mia asked, not looking up from her microscope.

Alex passed it over. "Your wish is my command, Dr. Chen."

"I'm not a doctor," she reminded him with a smirk.

"Just practicing for when you get that PhD. Besides, you've got the bossy part down already."

Mia tossed a crumpled sticky note at Alex, which he caught with surprising dexterity given his tremor. "Not bad for a guy who can't hold a coffee cup steady," she teased.

"I've developed very specific skills," Alex replied with a grin. "Coffee is expendable. Important data from beautiful scientists is not."

"Smooth talker. Is that how you charmed all those nurses in the ER?"

"Please. They were immune to my charms. Much like our zombie friends are immune to us."

The couple's laughter filled the lab as they continued working side by side. The easy rhythm of their banter matched the synchronicity of their movements.

"You know," Mia said, making a note in her research journal, "your theory about protein binding actually makes sense. For once."

"That's high praise coming from you. Should I mark the calendar for this historic moment?"

"Absolutely. Right next to 'Alex finally remembered to label his samples properly.'"

"That was one time!" he protested, his brown eyes sparkling.

"It was one very memorable time that cost us a week of work," Mia countered, her smile softening the critique.

Alex paused his work to look at her. "We make a good team, don't we?"

"The best," she agreed, meeting his eyes briefly before looking back down at her work, a slight blush coloring her cheeks.

They shared an easy silence, returning to their analysis. Their common purpose was clear in every careful measurement and recorded observation. An undeniable magnetism lurked beneath it too—one that neither was quite ready to acknowledge fully, but both were increasingly unable to ignore.

Furtive glances were exchanged across microscopes, and elbows lingered side by side adjusting equipment. Both denied a brewing attraction. But their sheer hours in close proximity eroded professional barriers. After draining testing days, they stayed up late chatting about fears and dreams beyond Parkinson's research. Their guards were lowered by fatigue, and the conversations ventured more and more into the abstract and emotional.

Mia confessed the isolation her childhood illness inflicted on her, the loneliness of suffering no one fully understood. Alex described losing his steadfast grandmother, forced to watch nine years of her erosion despite devoted care.

Something profound stirred in these shared revelations of personal battles fought largely solo by those now joined against the world's chaos. The intimacy of it created a refuge for two long-fortressed souls too accustomed to standing apart from even loved ones.

Furtive lab breakroom dinners evolved into long moonlit walks as Alex and Mia shared secrets and expressed dreams. The outside threats awaited their vigilance by day but released them come evening to wander where inspiration took them—both intellectual and emotional.

And always upon parting, a stare held a beat too long, bodies angled in sync, hinting more was left unspoken. Yet some currents pull even the sagest minds out to sea, and this spell between two unlikely kindred spirits suddenly grew into more than the sum of all they knew.

The walls between professional obligation and profound affinity were eroding daily. Even the noblest tenets of duty stood little chance against the timeless forces steadily drawing Alex and Mia into one another's orbit—two patient planets finally glimpsing light in the darkness.

One night close to midnight, Alex and Mia finally stepped outside after another marathon session poring over data sets and hypotheses. Exhausted but wired, they wandered the hospital grounds, leaves crunching underfoot—equal parts vigilance and release.

When an unexpected patrol light flashed in the darkness, adrenaline surged as they ducked for cover behind stacks of empty barrels. Alex pulled Mia tight as shouts faded into the distance. Alex knew he should release her, but he found himself transfixed, acutely aware of her quickened breath against his neck.

Mia looked up and smiled.

Alex saw her irrepressible brightness that he had so envied amidst their bleak days.

"Having you here gives me hope," Mia whispered. Her hand brushed Alex's cheek gently as the space between them electrified.

"I admire your resilience so much," Alex confessed, her zest for living a shining light with the world collapsing around them. Before doubts stalled him, he lowered his mouth to hers.

The kiss transported them from damp soil and rusting drums. Time stood still. Even nature's power paled beside the wellspring of tenderness and desire binding their separate lives into one.

Reluctantly they drew apart, foreheads touching as feet found earth again. Mia took Alex's hand in hers, turning toward the complex that both sheltered them and sealed their existence away from broader humanity.

At Mia's suite room door, Alex lingered, grip tightening around her graceful fingers—half request, half releasing to untenable forces. "I was under the impression we were going to keep this professional," she said gently.

Alex walked slowly to his own room, feeling her phantom lips still grazing his skin. Life amidst death had lit a dangerous flame inside him. But even reckless hope now felt essential to surviving the long road left.

Some greater compass than reason was charting his course across the wilderness now. The future beyond was obscured, but beside Mia the path was starting to emerge bright and clear. The rest would come or not. For now he savored the sweet unfolding, led onward through the dark by love's delicate, undeniable call.

Behind closed doors, they revealed their deepest hopes and fears, finding solace in each other's arms. With the world hunting them, each treasured moment could be their last. But their love dulled that pain, leaving only moments of passion and a profound trust like no other.

Their devotion to their work stayed true, but now Alex and Mia had even greater reason to persevere. They dared envision a future beyond this chaos, one they might share someday if they managed to survive this nightmare. For now, their love remained an oasis of light in the darkness—a glimmer of life and beauty persisting even at humanity's darkest hour.

Chapter 16: An Impossible Cure

Late one night, Sarah and Mia were testing a new series of antibody compounds against infected blood samples. The lab was quiet save for the gentle hum of equipment and the occasional sound of glass clinking against metal as Sarah and Mia worked. They'd been running assays for hours, testing various compounds against blood samples to understand the protective mechanisms at work.

"Can you hand me the next control sample?" Sarah asked, not looking up from her microscope. "We need to establish the baseline reaction before moving to the test compounds."

Mia nodded, moving to the refrigerated storage unit where their carefully labeled samples were kept. Her mind was elsewhere, though. Earlier that day, she'd noticed a slight tremor in her left hand that hadn't been there before. Was it stress? Fatigue? Or was her Parkinson's progressing faster than expected?

"Earth to Mia," Sarah called, a hint of sisterly teasing in her voice. "You okay over there?"

"Yeah, sorry," Mia replied, shaking away her worries. "Just thinking about the results from the last batch." She quickly scanned the rows of vials, each in its designated spot in the storage rack. Her eyes landed on what she thought was the healthy human control sample. Without double-checking the label, Mia grabbed it and brought it to Sarah. "Here's the healthy sample," she said, placing it in the rack beside Sarah's workstation.

Sarah nodded her thanks and proceeded with the protocol, carefully preparing the sample for analysis. She added the reagents, set the timer, and waited for the reaction to develop.

Minutes later, Sarah frowned at the readout on her screen. "That's strange," she muttered, adjusting the settings on her equipment.

"What's wrong?" Mia asked, moving to look over Sarah's shoulder.

"These readings. They're way off from what we'd expect in a healthy sample." Sarah's brow furrowed as she studied the results. "There's a significant decrease in dopamine transporter binding, and also there are elevated levels of alpha-synuclein aggregates."

Mia leaned in for a closer look, confusion giving way to realization as she spotted the label on the vial. "Oh no," she said, her voice barely above a whisper.

"What?" Sarah asked, looking up at her sister's stricken expression.

"I gave you the wrong sample," Mia admitted, pointing to the label. "That's *not* healthy blood. It's one of the Parkinson's samples."

Sarah stared at the vial for a long moment, then she looked back at the readings on her screen. She suddenly straightened, her eyes widening. "Wait a minute," she said slowly. "These readings ... the reaction we're seeing with our test compound ..."

Mia caught on immediately. "It's completely different than what we've seen before."

"The compound isn't just masking the Parkinson's signatures," Sarah said, excitement building in her voice. "It's actively *targeting* the alpha-synuclein deposits."

"Which means ..." Mia's voice trailed off, hardly daring to believe it.

"We might have stumbled onto something that doesn't just *mimic* Parkinson's immunity," Sarah said, quickly pulling up comparison data on her computer. The test results came back with highly irregular immune activity readings. "This could potentially modify the disease itself."

Mia's hands trembled as she grabbed her phone. "We need to tell Alex and Sam. Right now."

As Sarah hurriedly documented the unexpected results, Mia stared at the innocent-looking vial that might have just changed everything. Could her accidental mistake lead to the breakthrough they'd been searching for—not just protection from the infected, but possibly a treatment for Parkinson's itself?

The implications were staggering—and potentially dangerous. What had started as a simple error might upend everything they thought they knew about both Parkinson's disease and zombie immunity.

Mia ran to wake Alex. She quickly texted Sam on their group chat, "Video conference NOW!"

Meanwhile, Sarah initiated a new series of tests on the Parkinson's sample, anticipating they were on the brink of something huge. Mia and Alex came rushing in, with Alex bleary-eyed but alert.

Sarah showed them the strange results, like nothing she had seen from normal nor infected blood.

"What? Did you find the cure for Parkinson's?" Alex asked, rubbing the sleep from his eyes.

"Let's not get ahead of ourselves," Sam muttered on screen. "Trust and verify."

Sarah repeated the assays, controlled and confirmed, growing more excited. After so many grueling days stagnated by obstacles, this accidental discovery felt fated.

While the team analyzed the Parkinson's sample further, they had stumbled upon a compound that actually *reversed* Parkinson's symptoms. At first, they were stunned.

Could this truly be a cure? Alex wondered.

When the team repeated the tests, they confirmed the compound's restorative effects. Re-energized but also apprehensive, they threw themselves into fully analyzing this compound's properties, determined to find the right path forward.

Initially, they celebrated, knowing how many lives this could save from Parkinson's disease, including their own. But as the elation faded, a terrifying realization set in.

The euphoria of discovering a Parkinson's cure quickly curdled into dread as the unintended consequences became apparent. Eliminating the disease would strip away the serendipitous zombie immunity it granted. Releasing this cure could potentially render all of humanity detectable by the undead.

The lab was silent as Alex, Mia, and Sarah sat around the conference table with Sam watching on from Zoom, with the vial of what they now knew to be a potential Parkinson's cure sitting in the center like a time bomb.

Alex spoke first. "This feels impossible. We finally have what could be a cure for Parkinson's, but using it could literally doom humanity."

"My head is spinning in circles," Sam said, rubbing his forehead. "How do we choose? Either we withhold a cure from millions of suffering people, or we risk turning them all into zombie targets."

"I keep thinking about my aunt—how she suffered for years. What right do we have to keep this cure from people like her?" Mia asked.

"I get that, but what right do we have to make them vulnerable to the infected?" Sarah countered. "It's not just about individual choice when the consequences affect everyone."

"Maybe we could be selective?" Alex threw out. "Could we only offer it to people in the safest zones or to those with the most advanced symptoms?"

"So we play God? We decide who deserves to be cured and who doesn't?" Mia asked.

"What about modifying the cure?" Sam suggested. "Administering just enough to alleviate the worst symptoms while maintaining the camouflage effect?"

Sarah shook her head. "The initial tests suggest it's all or nothing. The same mechanism that cures the disease destroys the protection. We might be able to find a middle ground, but that would be months or even years of research away."

"And in the meantime, people keep suffering while we sit on a cure," Alex said.

"While others could die if we release it and they lose their immunity," Sam said.

After a long pause, Mia spoke. "What if we give people the choice? Full disclosure, full consent."

"But can anyone truly consent when the information is this incomplete?" the scientist in Sarah offered. "We don't even know if the immunity is permanent or if it varies in strength."

Alex sighed deeply. "We're going in circles. No option is perfectly right or completely wrong."

"Maybe that's the point. There *is* no perfect answer." Sam looked at Alex, overwhelmed.

"So what do we do right now?" Mia asked.

"We keep researching," her sister suggested. "We try to find that middle ground, even if it takes time."

"And in the meantime, we keep this secure. No publishing, no announcements," Alex said, looking at Sam.

"But we document everything, so that whatever happens, the knowledge isn't lost."

"And we stay true to why we started this in the first place—to help people, not harm them," Mia reminded.

"I can live with that for now," Alex said. "We keep searching for a better answer while protecting what we've found."

Sam nodded. "One step at a time. That's all we can do."

The four exchanged glances as the weight of their decision settled over them. No perfect solution existed, but they had found a path forward they could all accept—at least for now.

Alex leaned forward in his seat to pick up the vial. Turning the small container over in his shaky hand, he stared intently at the liquid within. As he grasped the vial, the enormity of its significance pressed heavily on him. This was no ordinary medication but a scientific breakthrough with consequences extending to all humanity.

Releasing this genie from its bottle could restore vibrant life to millions suffering from Parkinson's. But it could also unravel the inadvertent zombie immunity that might be humankind's only defense against extinction. Alex stood frozen at the threshold between deliverance and doom.

For a fleeting moment, Alex's memory returned him to his neurologist's office, where he sat reeling from his devastating diagnosis. He remembered his grandmother's steady decline and how his own creeping tremors and rigidity robbed him of dignity and control.

In Alex's tremoring hand, the promise of relief beckoned—freedom from unremitting suffering, a chance to reclaim his stolen future. He pressed his thumb to the vial cap, ready to savor that tranquility once more.

Then Alex's musings morphed to horror as he imagined zombies swarming unchecked through cities, the invisible cloak of Parkinson's having been ripped away. Screams echoed in his mind as humanity cowered defenseless, picked off until the last silenced heart.

Snapping back to reality, Alex tightened his grip on the vial, realizing how close he had come to opening Pandora's box in a moment of weakness. Lured by the faint glimmer of personal hope, he nearly unleashed calamity by one impulsive choice.

Alex knew a wise path would be found somewhere in this darkness, however obscured it was for now. He trusted that together with his friends, their moral compass would guide humanity through these impossible straits. Come what may, this awesome responsibility could not be borne alone.

Consumed by the moral dilemma before him, Alex was deaf to the world, oblivious to anything other than the vial he clutched in his trembling hand. The weight of this discovery felt like his alone to bear, a Sisyphean ordeal.

Alex became aware of two sets of hands resting gently but firmly on his shoulders. The warm touch pulled Alex from his anguished trance. He lifted his eyes to see Sarah and Mia looking back, their expressions radiating compassion.

In that moment, words were unnecessary. The faces of his friends reminded Alex that no matter the obstacles ahead, he did not have to face them alone. He knew that their steadfast loyalty would sustain him through the impossible trials still to come.

Alex's lips curled into a weary smile as he reached up to clasp their hands in silent gratitude. Stormy weather often illuminates the strongest anchors. Alex's trust in human bonds stilled his spirit even amidst overwhelming forces.

United by this journey, the team shared the weight of decisions that now extended far beyond themselves. But anchored in their human connection, no challenge felt insurmountable. Where answers elude even the wise, love lights the way.

The debate remained unfinished, but clearer heads now prevailed. Having come so far and sacrificed so much, the irony was not lost on them. But out of life's infinite complexity, there is always hope of finding unity through compassion. Where both seem impossible, often it is human bonds that show us how.

Chapter 17: On the Run

Over the next few weeks, the team became increasingly worried that the authorities were onto their clandestine research and secret breakthrough. Alex and Mia were known Parkies, who were now required to be registered with the government, due to the apparent link between PD and zombie immunity. The authorities were also suspicious of people with medical backgrounds. They knew there was research being conducted at various underground labs around the country, and they were especially targeting people with *both* PD and a medical background.

One day, Alex was called to a downtown government building for an interrogation. The two rough-looking agents' line of questioning quickly turned hostile. They asked what he was doing in Ann Arbor, they clearly knew he was from New York, and they were very curious about his history of close calls with the zombies. The interrogators probed Alex, explaining that they heard speculation about a compound curing the zombies and cloaking people.

Under intense scrutiny, Alex revealed sparse details about discovering a Parkinson's cure, but he insisted that further testing was required given its unpredictable side effects. "The looming consequences are too perilous to rush," he explained.

"I'm this close to charging you with withholding vital public health knowledge during a crisis!" the older of the agents threatened.

But Alex refused to relent. Too many lives were at stake to trust blind hopes over careful science.

By the time Alex returned to the University of Michigan campus, Sam, back at his own office, had noticed digital chatter erupting about them. Sam's algorithms tracked their names suddenly appearing on restricted law enforcement bulletins.

"Get out of that lab NOW!" Sam texted in their group chat.

Urgently, Alex, Mia, and Sarah had gathered their essential research and slipped out of the lab—moments before a SWAT team swarmed it.

Suddenly, the team were enemies of the state by virtue of due diligence, with no rights or recourse remaining to them. They were now on the run.

Over the next few weeks, state lines and seedy motels blurred together. Paranoia became Alex, Mia, and Sarah's boon companion. Burner phones, forged IDs, and cobbled-together disguises became their off-grid tool kit. They jumped from hotel to hotel, never staying more than one night before disappearing again like ghosts.

One night in yet another seedy motel, a breaking news bulletin flashed urgently across the motel room's grainy TV: "Scientists allegedly developed a cure for the mysterious infected pandemic, but they've disappeared after refusing to cooperate with federal authorities."

Alex shot up from his half-sleep to see his photo flash on screen with photos of Mia and Sarah—along with video of smoldering ruins of their lab. He muted the broadcast and exchanged tense looks with Mia and Sarah. How long did they have before the manhunt closed around them?

Exhausted and isolated by their life on the run, Alex, Mia, and Sarah drew closer. Their friendship was now all that remained certain amidst swirling chaos. They were united by bonds beyond worlds that refused to understand. They clasped hands tightly, steeling for whatever new battle awaited come dawn. For now, solidarity and sleep.

Week after week, Alex, Mia, and Sarah managed to remain undetected by the authorities hunting them. Each night, they took refuge in a different dingy, cash-only motel, avoiding leaving a trail that could reveal their location.

During the days, the trio constantly relocated too, hiding in plain sight reading newspapers at all-night diners, shuffling in gray hoodies through bustling hospitals where they went unnoticed in the chaos. They mastered the art of blending into the background, becoming ghosts in a landscape that no longer welcomed their existence.

It was a grinding, paranoid way to exist, but they had no choice. They were grateful for Sam across the country, who scanned encrypted channels for digital whispers about their case. But it seemed the manhunt had moved elsewhere for now. Still they knew one tiny misstep could betray their presence, so vigilance held its grip tight.

When the team's funds dwindled, they tapped contacts from Alex's long forgotten past, who helped discreetly shuttle cash and essentials to wherever the fugitive trio temporarily took roost. Old debts long dissolved came repaid when Alex's former patients got word of his plight.

Day after day, they endured this transient purgatory, relying on obscurity while continuing their research out of briefcases and diner booths. It was far from ideal, but their inputs were untraceable, results undetectable from remote servers. Progress inched slowly ahead despite their fractured existence.

Someday they hoped to resurface when their discovery could safely shield both Parkinson's and humankind together. Until then, they continued to hide in plain sight, letting the ghosts of better lives propel their steps forward. One sunrise soon, the running would cease. But not yet.

Chapter 18: Staying the Course

One day, pure exhaustion seeped through every cell of Alex's battered body as the trio took temporary refuge in a ramshackle barn. The past weeks spent fleeing authorities' endless reach had drained their mental fortitude down to the dregs. Each new day now felt like a hollowed-out vessel just trying to slip past unseen through another checkpoint, averting watchful eyes searching for any cracks in their armor.

Earlier, the endless stress boiled over when Alex froze entering a routine security stop. Mia, sensing the turbulence behind his eyes, quickly threw a ragged blanket she carried over his trembling form, obscuring him as one of the infected cadavers they transported for disposal. With rancid smells masking his human warmth, the guard grimaced and motioned them through without a second glance.

As they narrowly escaped once again, nerves frayed but intact, the absurd risks they now endured just to take another step weighed heavy. Returning to civil life was unfathomable, with government powers likely authorized to permanently silence their dissent. But even steadfast determination wavered against this relentless siege.

In the brief respite this drafty shelter provided, Alex slumped dejectedly onto a bed of moldy hay, fitful half-sleep his only balm. He felt Mia studying him with tender concern through the darkness, her delicate caresses barely registering through his numb exhaustion. Until their truth could emerge into daylight once more, the choice was either to persist in embattled solitude or fully relinquish themselves to obliteration.

In the musty barn that seemed worlds removed from society's crushing chaos, Alex finally exhaled, letting the full weight of despair overcome his stoic facade. How much farther could they flee before their heart or soul simply gave out? Would the next close call finally strip their fragile luck bare?

Sarah seemed to read Alex's inner turmoil. Through bloodshot eyes, she acknowledged the fatigue threatening to swallow them whole between shallow breaths. "Part of me doubts any future awaits us beyond this purgatory," she conceded. "Except what we've already resigned ourselves to ..."

Her unspoken meaning hung heavy between them. Their truth had already cost the lives of far nobler souls now a decade gone. Perhaps fading anonymously into obscure peace held more honor than waiting out their numbered days panting through death's creeping door.

But Mia clutched Alex fiercely, as if her will alone could root him to this. "That's what they want," she urged. "For us to fade quietly so their power faces no reckoning." Her eyes begged Alex not to relinquish their flickering torch lighting the abyss ahead. Not when they had sacrificed so much already. Their truth depended on it.

Alex kissed Mia solemnly in return. Come daybreak, they would summon what faint reserves remained to brave the hostile terrain again. Too many haunting dreams still preyed on the altars of their conscience. Until breath failed for the final time or redemption at last arrived, they would soldier on, emboldened by glory greater than self.

Sarah squeezed Alex's shoulder, taking the first watch between the creaking rafters. Whatever fuel yet burned inside would spark their lead through this pitch again. Beyond that lay only surrender. Mia wrapped Alex in her arms, shielding his fitful dreams from encroaching storms. Tomorrow they would make their exodus unbroken once more.

As the howling wind whipped around the decrepit barn, the storm's growing fury echoed their own beaten spirits. The elements' rage would mask them a while longer, but morning's light threatened fresh persecution.

Curled against Alex, Mia hummed a familiar lullaby to soothe his restless mind from constantly scanning the shadows for new threats. Her melody cut through the wailing gusts outside, kindling a moment's respite where Alex could release his frayed nerves after weeks running unchecked.

In Mia's arms, the weary miles ahead faded briefly until only this shelter remained—two souls cleaving together amidst chaos. Eyes closed, Alex briefly forgot the impossible labyrinth looming ever nearer. He focused instead on Mia's delicate heartbeat against his chest, willing it to infuse new life into his depleted reserves.

Alex knew their humanitarian vow had likely condemned them to follow this lonesome road into oblivion. Every faint cry echoing the forsaken wilderness beckoned them further. Without Mia's persevering spirit lighting the path ahead, Alex feared his legs might finally falter. Her steadfast devotion fueled his own when so little kindling remained inside to spark purpose anymore.

Outside the winds raged on, seasonal in their cycles of fury and calm. But humans could walk only so far stretched to their limits before the last embers of hope guttered out. Alex clung to slumber, praying dawn might reignite the cause. Until then, he allowed himself to drift in Mia's hold, stirred by her unwavering voice calling him back from the void.

As they lay together in the stillness, the storm raging outside provided a strange comfort—its chaos masking their presence from those who sought them.

Mia's humming gradually stopped, and Alex felt her body tense slightly against his.

"What is it?" he whispered, his voice barely audible above the wind.

She was quiet for a moment before answering. "I've been thinking about my patients—the ones in the nursing home before all this started."

Alex shifted to face her in the darkness, their faces close. "The Parkinson's patients?"

"Yes," Mia nodded, a heaviness in her voice. "I watched them deteriorate day by day. Helped them eat when their hands wouldn't cooperate. Cleaned them when they couldn't make it to the bathroom in time. Held them when they cried from frustration."

"You were there for them," Alex said gently. "That matters."

"But I never truly understood," Mia whispered, her voice breaking. "Not until I felt my own hands starting to betray me. The way people look at you when they notice. The pity, the discomfort. It's different when you're a woman too."

"Different how?"

Mia sighed. "Men with tremors are seen as distinguished, maybe just overworked. Women are seen as nervous, hysterical. I had doctors dismiss my early symptoms, tell me it was just anxiety." She laughed bitterly. "As if I hadn't spent years recognizing Parkinson's symptoms in others."

A long silence stretched between them, filled only by the howling of the wind. Alex noticed something different about the way Mia held herself—a steadiness that hadn't been there before.

"I need to tell you something," Mia finally said, her voice clear and steady. "I did something."

Alex waited, sensing the weight of her confession.

"Before we left the lab..." Mia took a deep breath. "I took some of the serum—the one that cures Parkinson's."

Alex stiffened beside her. "Mia—"

"I used it, Alex. Three days ago."

Alex pulled back, trying to see her face in the darkness. "What? But the immunity—"

"Is gone. I know," she said quietly. "I'm vulnerable now, like everyone else."

"Why would you risk that?" Alex asked, his voice a mix of confusion and fear. "After everything we've learned. After everything we're fighting for!"

"Because I couldn't bear it anymore," she admitted. "Watching my body fail me bit by bit, knowing what was coming. I've seen the end of this road too many times with my patients. I couldn't walk it myself, not when I had a choice."

"But now you're in danger. If the infected—"

"I know the risks," she interrupted. "But for the first time in years, my hands don't shake. My muscles don't freeze. I can move, think, exist without the constant reminder that my body is betraying me." Mia reached out to touch Alex's face, her movements fluid and precise. "Can you understand that?"

Alex was silent, processing her revelation.

"I'm still me, Alex. Still committed to our work. We're determined to find a way to protect everyone. But I needed to save myself first." Her voice broke slightly. "Please don't hate me for it."

Alex pulled Mia close again, his emotions conflicted. "I could never hate you. I just ... I'm scared for you now."

"I know. But I'll be careful." Mia pressed her forehead against Alex's. "And you'll protect me, just like I've protected you."

They fell back into silence, the implications of her decision hanging between them. The storm outside began to subside as dawn approached. In a few hours, they would need to move again, continuing their dangerous journey with a new vulnerability among them. But for now, in this moment of raw honesty, they clung to each other—one freed from disease but exposed to new dangers, the other still trapped in his deteriorating body but shielded from the world's most immediate threat.

Outside, the winds raged on, indifferent to the human choices made in desperate times.

About the Author

Eric Aquino is a first-generation American born to parents who emigrated from the Dominican Republic. He grew up in Jersey City in a large, close-knit family. From a young age, Eric was drawn to helping others, often being called upon to assist and translate for family members.

After initially wanting to become a lawyer, Eric earned a bachelor's degree in Information Technology, but he remained committed to helping people. In 2002, he moved to Pennsylvania, and at a friend's suggestion he began volunteering as an EMT. This experience ignited Eric's passion, and he knew he wanted to pursue a career in emergency services.

While working in the ER at Easton Hospital in 2007, Eric met a charge nurse who was diagnosed with stage 4 breast cancer, and he wanted to show his support. He reconnected with a high school friend and signed up for the Avon Breast Cancer Walk in New York in 2009. Eric continued participating in the walk for the next nine years, raising $1,800 annually.

In 2018, at age 40, Eric was diagnosed with Parkinson's disease. Determined to help others facing the same challenges, he founded the Gray Strong Foundation that fall. Over the next six years, Eric started three support groups, hosted three symposiums, presented a poster at the World Parkinson's Congress in Barcelona, and participated on panels at various symposiums—all with the mission of helping people with Parkinson's move forward with their lives.